love among

th

Book One

In Dublin

Fair City

M. KATHERINE CLARK

ISBN-13: 978-0-9998708-6-0

Other Works by M. Katherine Clark

The Greene and Shields Files
  Blood is Thicker Than Water
  Once Upon a Midnight Dreary
  Old Sins Cast Long Shadows
  Tales from the Heart, *Novelettes*
Love Among the Shamrocks Collection
  Under the Irish Sky
  Across the Irish Sea
  On the River Shannon
  Land Across the Sea, *an Emmet O'Quinn Short Story*
Love Among the Shamrocks Collection: The Next Generation
  In Dublin Fair City
  The Song of Heart's Desire
  Chasing After Moonbeams – *Coming Soon*
The Wolf's Bane Saga
  Wolf's Bane
  Lonely Moon
  Midnight Sky
  Star Crossed
  Moon Rise
  Moon Song, *a companion guide*
Soundless Silence, *a Sherlock Holmes Novel*
The Rest is Silence, *an Edmond Holmes Novel* – *Coming Soon*
Silent Whispers, *a Scottish Ghost Story*
Dragon Fire
  Heart of Fire
  Will of Fire – *Coming Soon*

For my mother. Thank you for introducing all types of music to me, but especially musicals and opera. I will always credit you for my love of music!

Prologue

Trinity College Dublin

He looked around the opulent theater lobby seeing other guests in tuxes, ball gowns, and masks of varying styles. There were delicate masks, traditional black silk masks, doctor's masks from the time of the plague with their long noses and intricate designs, comedy-tragedy masks, colorful masks, masks that covered the entire face, the top half, or the side, animal masks, character masks, scary masks, elegant masks, anything one could think of, danced, mingled, and drank all around him.

He glanced down at his modern tuxedo. The jacket was fitted, a mark from his grandfather always telling him, a well-fitted suit told a lot about a man, and a white button up shirt, lined with a strip of black silk, and black round buttons. He had debated for nearly twenty minutes if he wanted to wear a tie, bowtie, or leave the top two buttons undone. Eventually, time was the determining factor and as he slipped on his black, red, and gold Venetian mask, he had tossed the strip of black that hung around his neck onto his bed and left his flat.

Standing in the Trinity College theater holding a glass of whiskey, hearing the music, and seeing the dancers pair off, he dampened his nerves. The fifteen-foot Christmas tree stood off to the side near the bar decorated in gold, red, and green and of course their school colors of cool blue and steel grey lined the bar. The ivory walls were covered in ornate gold ormolus of vines, leaves, and pillar crowns. Beautiful statues of Greek gods looked down on him and he remembered how he felt the first time he stepped into the theater. It was breathtaking.

After a moment of admiration, he felt the hair on the back of his neck stand on end. Turning to the grand stair, he saw her. She stood at the top of the staircase, her off the shoulder sweetheart neckline red dress popped against the ivory-gold of the wall behind her. Her delicate Venetian swan mask gracefully covered the top part of her face, coming down to the middle of her nose, the left side fanned up like a swan's wing. She looked stunning, just the way he knew she would. Their eyes locked and he saw the flicker of surprise then the heat of a blush flushed her cheeks. But he caught no hint of recognition.

Good, all is going according to plan, he thought.

She started down the stairs, her eyes never leaving his. The side of his mouth ticked up as he saw the quick rise and fall of her chest and the flush coloring her neck. She stood two steps above him, but they were eye to eye, and she had yet to drop his gaze. It was now or never. Taking a deep breath, he channeled his father's deeper and heavily Irish accented voice to disguise his own.

"I've been waiting for you," he stated.

"Me?" she questioned.

"Aye," he replied, happy with his impersonation.

"Why? Do I know you?"

"Wouldn't you know me, if you did?"

"There's a lot of students here," she answered, and he smiled at her slight American accent. "Your mask is brilliant and covering most of your face. If I'm supposed to, I'm sorry," she shook her head, then her eyes narrowed. "There is something"

"Something?"

"Familiar... I feel like I do know you. What's your name? Take off the mask?" She reached up to remove it, but he gently caught her wrist stopping her.

He shook his head. "No, Cassie," he said. "You don't need to know me, yet."

"Please?"

"Dance with me," he offered.

She stared at him again for a long moment. "Why do I get the feeling my life will change depending on the answer?"

He said nothing, just placed his empty glass on the tray of a passing waiter and offered his hand to her. Cassie looked at the hand, then him.

"Please, tell me your name."

He thought a moment and when he heard the orchestral start playing *Music of the Night* from the *Phantom of the Opera*, he nodded.

"You can call me Phantom."

"Phantom?" she questioned with a grin. "That's not a name."

"It's enough of one," he replied. "Trust me."

"Trust is easy to come by, but a second chance rarely happens."

3

He said nothing for a long moment waiting for her to slip her hand into his. She didn't hesitate. Walking over to the dancefloor, he took her hand and placed his other on the small of her back. In that moment, he was eternally grateful to his stepmother for teaching him how to dance.

The tempo was slow, and they danced together not speaking but never dropping each other's gazes.

"I've always cared for you, Cassie. I need you to know that. I suppose I am concerned about your reaction so that is why I do not tell you who I am. I don't mean to scare you or anything like that, but I have to tell you... I love you. I have for a couple years now. And aye, I'm not some stalker. You do know me. I even can claim the distinction of being a friend."

"I have several friends."

"I know," he answered. "That is why I am not being any more specific. Just know, if you need me, I'll always be there for you."

"How will I know how I feel if you don't tell me who you are? I could very easily be in love with you."

"Give me a task. Anything. I will do what you ask and come to you without the mask, only me and you can decide then if you want me or not."

Cassie stared into his eyes and just as the music climaxed, she nodded.

"Okay, Phantom," she smiled. "I have something I want you to get for me."

"Name it and it's yours."

Chapter

One

Five Months Later

Trevor O'Quinn looked up and across the lawn toward the entrance to the Old Library of Trinity College in Dublin to see his half-brother and sister rushing over to him. There on a visit to see if it was where they wanted to go to school, Killian and Aoife laughed together before breathlessly coming to a stop in front of him.

Trevor smiled and closed the music book he was studying, stood from the park bench, and hugged his younger siblings.

"Well?" He asked. "How was it?"

"The tour was okay," Killian started, "But since I had

already seen everything with da', it was somewhat boring."

"Same," Aoife replied. "But Uni guys are hot."

"Aoife," Trevor warned. "You're sixteen. You don't know what hot means... right?"

She just giggled at his overprotective brotherliness and continued. "I wish you could have joined us."

"I know, guys, I'm sorry. I had class," he explained. "But, hey, let's go across the way and get some coffee."

Aoife made a cute disgusted sound. "You know I don't drink that stuff. Icky black ink."

"Blame the American in me," Trevor winked. "I can't get enough of the stuff."

"Da' says we'll have to learn to love it when we go to University," Killian answered as they walked toward the archway exit to the little coffee shop near campus.

"Da' is right," Trevor replied. "When you spend all night studying and have an eight am class, trust me, coffee is a lifesaver."

Waiting until it was safe to cross the street, Trevor took a moment to watch his twin brother and sister and smiled. It had been seventeen years since he and his father Emmet and stepmom Mara had left America to go back to Ireland and though those first two years Trevor barely understood what was going on at his *Gaelscoil,* he was happy to be in his father's homeland. But soon, with his Uncle Sean's tutelage, he was able to excel and was accepted to one of the finest schools in the world, his father's *Alma Mater,* Trinity College in Dublin.

Since they moved back, his cousins both older and younger had been his best friends, at least until his twin younger brother and sister were born. Then he had the siblings he always wanted. They had been close ever since.

"Trev?" Aoife's voice cleared his mind and he focused on his siblings standing on the other side of the road. He gave an awkward laugh and wave then hurriedly crossed the street.

"Sorry," he said. "My mind drifted."

"Everything okay?" Killian asked.

"Yeah sorry, honestly I was thinking about my first few years here in Ireland. It's nothing."

"We're definitely glad you, Mum, and Da' came back. I can't imagine growing up anywhere else," Aoife said.

"American isn't bad," Trevor replied.

"No, just, there's nothing like Ireland," she clarified.

"I'm right there with you," Trevor agreed.

They pushed the door open and stepped into the coffee shop. The smell of freshly ground coffee and chocolate assaulted their noses. Trevor took a deep breath and smiled, letting out a satisfied sound.

"My grampa always says there's nothing like the smell of fresh grounds," he said.

"No, thank you," Aoife teased. "I'll take a hot chocolate."

"One hot chocolate and a spiced orange cake, got it," he winked. "Can you get us a table?"

She nodded and with a thank you, she headed to a four topper by the window. Trevor and Killian stood together in line at the café.

"So, what do you think?" Trevor asked.

"What about?" Killian replied.

"About college? Have you told Mum and Dad what you told

7

me?"

Killian's eyes grew large as he glanced around to make sure no one heard him.

"Please," he started. "I told you that in confidence."

"I'm not going to say anything, but don't you think you need to tell them soon? You only have two more years until college. They should know before then."

Killian huffed a sigh and ran his hand through his dark brown hair, his ice blue eyes begged him.

"I don't know what to do," he admitted. "I feel like such a failure. Da' has so many plans. He wants me to do so much and I…"

"Hey," Trevor turned to face his brother. "Don't go there. You are your own person and our parents love you. They'll be okay."

"They'll not be very happy with my choice," he shrugged.

"Trust me, I know what that's like," Trevor clapped his brother on the shoulder. "I'll be with you, if you want. When you tell them."

His young face lit with hope. "Will you?"

"Of course! I'd be happy to," Trevor grinned. "I know how it can be to tell our parents something you think will change how they look at you but trust me, it won't. They love you."

"You know?"

"You remember the year I took off between final year and college? When I travelled with my grandparents?" At Killian's nod, he continued. "I was worried because da' did that too when he was my age and always regretted it. Said no matter how amazing his travels were, it threw the timing off. But when I told him, he was fine. Said it was my choice, my life to choose what I should do. He supported me."

"But you *went* to college… it's not the same," Killian grumbled.

"'Tis," Trevor stressed. "Anyway, enough about that. What do you want?" He indicated the menu hanging overhead. They were next in line and Killian studied the board. Once he told him and Trevor ordered, they waited for the drinks and took the number for the food. Meeting their sister at the table, she put her phone down and took her hot chocolate.

"Cheers, Trev," she leaned back in the wooden chair and took a sip.

"Careful, it'll be hot," Trevor cautioned.

"Scalding," she giggled and set it down, dabbing her eyes as tears formed.

"You all right?" he asked.

"Fine," she promised. "Just an idiot."

"We knew that," her twin winked.

"Lay off," Aoife laughed and took a glass of the ice water Trevor had ordered. "So, what were you guys talking about? It looked important."

Trevor didn't react but Killian's eyes grew wide and he looked at both of his siblings.

"Uh oh," Aoife leaned forward. "This looks fun. What happened?"

Aoife's large blue eyes danced; a finer point of her facial expressions learned directly from her mother; Mara. But the ice blue eyes were distinctly from their father, Emmet.

Trevor sighed and leaned back in his chair with his coffee.

"If you really must know—"

"Oh, I must," she answered.

"I told Killian a secret," Trevor started.

"I like secrets," Aoife said.

"What I'm planning for my recital," he lied.

"Oh," she looked dejected. "That's it?"

"What do you mean, *that's it?*" Trevor chuckled. "It's a big deal."

"I was hoping for something a little more... juicy," she said.

"Juicy?" Trevor laughed. "So sorry to disappoint."

Aoife sighed and leaned back. "So, what are you planning? Final year recital is pretty big right?"

"'Tis," he answered as they accepted the two slices of cake he ordered from the barista. "Some talent scouts for master degree program usually come and it's my grade for several classes."

"How?" She asked digging into her favorite orange spiced cake.

"Not only singing but stage presence, aural skills, theory, and piano performance. They want to see it all. It's nerve-wracking. They throw shite at you just to see how you respond. One of my best friends last year was set to be best in his class and when they threw a choir back up and gave him a Mozart piece to sight read..." Trevor shook his head. "He ended up being about twentieth in his class. He warned me to be at the top of everything and be prepared for the most unexpected thing."

"Like a choir backup on a Mozart piece," Killian said. "From my limited knowledge, it's unusual. Normally Mozart is either choir or solo hardly any sort of mixing."

"You're right. Not unheard of obviously but not usual."

"So, what's this surprise you're cooking up?" his sister asked.

"I'm going to anticipate them and do something no one else has done."

"What's that?"

"You'll have to wait and see," he winked.

"No fair! You told our brother! What, is he your favorite?"

"I don't have favorites," he teased.

"So…"

Trevor looked at Killian. "Should I tell her?"

Killian shook his head, a devilish smirk on his lips. Trevor looked back at their sister and shrugged. Aoife kicked them under the table.

"Ow," Trevor bent down to rub his shin. "Damn, Aoife."

"That's what you get for not telling me," she pouted. After a second of both brothers laughing at her antics, she continued. "It's next weekend, right?"

"Saturday," Trevor nodded. "I'm ready just to get it over with."

"I bet," she said. "I don't think I could ever be a singer. The things you and Mum have to do? Getting out on stage in front of people?" she shuddered. "Scary."

"It can be," he shrugged. "But when it's something you love to do; it just makes it easy."

"Trevor?" a woman's voice called from behind him. He

tried to prevent the instant smile that lifted his lips when he recognized the voice. Turning, he stood.

"Hey, Cassie," he greeted.

"Hey! How have you been? I swear I haven't seen you at all since we started this final session." she hugged him. He took a second to take a deep inhale of her perfume. She always smelled amazing. And that perfume meant something more to him. He remembered the one time he had searched high and low for it only to realize his main competition for Cassie's affections, Robbie McConaghy, heir apparent to his daddy's whiskey empire, had bought it for her and gave it to her first, successfully cutting him off.

Before he could reply, the said bastard, Robbie himself showed up and laid claim to her by an arm wrapped around her shoulders.

"There you are, baby," he said. Trevor caught her grimace.

"Yeah, hey," she answered. "I saw Trevor and wanted to say hello."

"Leave the Yank alone, you promised me lunch before our next class and I'm looking forward to dessert," he licked the shell of her ear, his eyes on Trevor.

The message was clear, *back off.*

Cassie forced a smile. "I'll see you later, Trev?" she asked.

"Yeah sure," he answered. Robbie gave him his trademarked smarmy smile saying *not going to happen.* Trevor watched them go.

Having meet Cassie his first year at Trinity, they latched on to each other when they learned their mothers were American and Trevor had yet to fully adopt an Irish accent from having lived the first few years of his life in America. Cassie's accent was subtle since she was born in Ireland but had an American accent at home while she was growing up. Sometimes she used Americanisms only Trevor and the other small handful of undergraduates from America understood. Their friendship grew over the last three years until Robbie wheedled his way in between them.

Watching them leave the café, Trevor huffed a sigh and turned back to his siblings.

"What was that?" Aoife asked.

"Hmm? Oh, um, a friend. Cassie," he sat down.

"Not her, the wanker," Aoife said.

"Aoife," Trevor scolded. "Mum will blame me if she hears you speaking like that."

"Tosh, ma knows it's da' not you. Besides, if ever there was an appropriate use for that term, it would be him."

"I agree, Trev," Killian said. "He basically licked her, claiming she was his."

"Well, they've been dating since Christmas so I would assume she is his," Trevor replied taking a drink of his coffee.

"A woman doesn't belong to a man," Aoife stated.

"That's not what I mean, Aoife and I agree with you," he said.

Aoife paused, looking over her now cooled hot chocolate, observing her brother.

"You like her," she deduced.

Trevor paused. It was on the tip of his tongue to deny it but he swore he would always be truthful with them so they would always feel comfortable coming to him with anything. Taking a deep breath, he let it out slowly.

"Aye, Aoife, I like her a lot."

"Then why do you allow him to treat her that way?"

"It's not my choice, nor is it my job to protect her. She's dating him. She chose him. There's nothing I can do."

"Bollocks," Killian replied. "You always taught me to fight for what I want. Hell, da' tells us all the time… literally… all… the… time how he had to fight for Mum. How would he feel if he knew his eldest son wasn't fighting for something he loves and wants?"

"I don't love her," Trevor defended.

"Maybe," Aoife said.

"Poor use of words," Killian replied at the same time. "What I mean is, you like her, and *he* clearly thinks of her as a possession."

"She likes you too," Aoife interjected.

"And she likes you too," Killian acquiesced. "You should give it a try."

"Leave it to my *younger* siblings to tell me what I should do with a woman," Trevor shook his head.

"We're not telling you anything Da' hasn't said before," Aoife laughed.

Killian's and Aoife's phones buzzed at the same time making them jump.

"Shite," Aoife cursed. "We got to go. The next tour is starting in ten."

Trevor drained his mug and set it on the tray. "Let's go then."

"You don't have to walk us across the street, Trev. We're fine. Finish the coffee in the carafe. We'll see you at dinner. You're still able to meet us for dinner, right?"

"Absolutely, I'll meet you at the pub across from my flat. My last class ends at four-thirty. The tour should be over around that time."

"We have a Q&A from four-thirty 'til five so we might be late, but we'll see you around then!" Aoife threw the last few words over her shoulder as she and Killian rushed out of the café.

Trevor chuckled remembering when he went on his first college visit to a different college in Galway where his cousin Fiona was studying technology and computer science. The tour guides were sticklers for punctuality.

Pouring the last of the coffee in his mug, he hummed a song, one in his repertoire the judges might ask for and pulled out his theory prep book. Turning to the last page of the notes section, he added another little idea to his list for the recital. He wanted to surprise the judges. Knowing everyone else would be reactive to what they said, he wanted to be proactive. Maybe it was the American in him but whatever it was, he enjoyed toying with a few ideas on how to beat them at their own game.

Chapter Two

The next day flew by as everyone on campus was getting ready for their final exams and the music school worked on their juried finals. With everything piling up, Trevor hadn't had a chance to call his dad for a couple days. Something he did every evening and as he fell into bed after midnight, he pulled out his phone and clicked over to his dad's text chain.

For the first few years of his life, Emmet O'Quinn had been a larger than life unattainable entity but when his mother died, his father moved with him to America. To this day, Trevor could not remember his mother, but he missed her more than he thought possible. Those four years he and his father spent together in America were an elusive memory, but it built the foundation of their relationship. His dad became more than a dad, he was his best friend and confidant. They moved back to Ireland and Emmet and Trevor's stepmother Mara renewed their vows, but Emmet made sure Trevor was still his number one priority.

When Mara's band *Celtic Spirit* went on tour, it was only Emmet and Trevor again for a short time. But when he was on summer break, Emmet would pack Trevor up and they would meet Mara on the road in America, Australia, France, Germany, Italy, wherever she was touring, and those memories made him smile.

The birth of his twin siblings, Killian and Aoife had put an end to their travels for a time. When they were born Mara took a break from singing for three years, then went on a comeback tour but by then, Trevor was twelve and able to help his father be a stay-at-home dad. When Mara's album went platinum, Emmet took less and less time at the dealership he owned. Soon, he sold it to Trevor's Uncles Paddy and Tom, Keera's and Chloe's husbands.

It was Mara who inspired Trevor to pursue his own singing career and even had him in the studio with her occasionally. Mara always treated him as her own son even though Trevor's mother, Jennifer had died when he was two.

When one of Mara's songs came over his headphones, he smiled but as her hauntingly beautiful voice sang *Raglan Road*, tears gathered in his eyes.

This was the time of year he hated the most. He hadn't been back home to Kerry since the new year and he missed his family. All of them. Two dozen cousins, his aunts and uncles, his Grandma Dee, and Grandad Orin. He missed his Aunt Charlotte and Uncle Derek and his cousin Peter back in America and especially his gramma and grampa, his mother's parents.

He missed his old dog too. His dad had kept the promise me made to get him a dog and took him to the pound to pick out his new pet. The memory of the old slobbery face of his lab-terrier mix crossed his mind and as sad as it was to lose him three years ago, he was so happy to have the sweet memories. Emmet had buried him next to his old lab, Jacks in his grandparent's backyard.

His throat closed with emotion. Letting out an irritated grunt, Trevor wiped his tears away and turned back to his text chain with his father.

Trevor: Hey, dad, sorry I've been MIA for a couple days and couldn't call you back. I hope everything is okay. I know you would have left a message if it wasn't. Miss you and Mum. Miss talking to you but with final exams and jury coming up, my life has been eat, sleep and study... though seeing the time it's more eat and study, than sleep. Anyway, miss you, hope to talk to you soon. No need to call or text back, I know you're probably asleep. Love you. Night.

Almost before Trevor set his phone down to charge, his dad's face popped up on the screen along with his special ringtone. Trevor smiled and answered the video call. His father's face filled the screen, his ice blue eyes and red hair, so similar to Trevor's, he grinned.

"Hiya, dad."

"Oh, Trev, it's good to see you, son. How are you? How's things? How's school?" Emmet asked.

"Good, yeah, busy. Did I wake you?" Trevor asked trying to ignore how much he wanted one of his dad's hugs telling him everything would be all right.

"Nah, I was up. Watching a scary movie with your mum who fell asleep on me, so now I'm checking every door and window to make sure it's locked."

Trevor chuckled. "It's the Irish countryside, dad. What evil monsters could be lurking there?"

"Aye, well, you'll never guess where this movie took

place."

"The Irish Countryside?" he guessed.

"Aye," Emmet chuckled then paused near the dining room window and turned his full attention on his son. "You doing all right, lad?"

Trevor nodded. "Just miss you."

"I miss you too, but I'll be seeing you on Saturday."

"Can't wait."

"How's things, though? Killian said he and Aoife had a great time visiting you and Trinity. It would be nice to have all my children go there."

Trevor debated but decided it was best. "You know, dad..." he started. "You might want to think of other options for them."

"Other options? Like what?"

"Like the possibility one or both may not want to go to college."

Emmet was quiet and Trevor kicked himself seeing understanding in his father's eyes. He should never have said anything. His brother may never forgive him.

"I wondered why he went. Your mother and I both know he doesn't want to go and hasn't told us yet. I'm glad he confided in you. I just hate the idea he won't get a degree. In today's job market an undergraduate degree is required for most good paying jobs."

"What do you mean?" Trevor questioned.

"Mara and I have known for a while Killian was looking at alternatives instead of university. We haven't said anything to him, hoping he would come to us himself, but he hasn't yet."

"Maybe mention in passing that it's all right not to go? That you wouldn't be disappointed in him," Trevor offered.

"I could never be disappointed in any of my children. Does he honestly think that?"

"I know nothing," Trevor replied. "I've already said too much."

"Of course," Emmet agreed. "I'm glad he knows he can confide in you. I'll say nothing about you mentioning it to me."

"Only because I worry about him."

"We both do, he's sixteen, you remember how it was back then."

"God, do I ever," Trevor chuckled. "It was brutal."

"It was for me too, yeah," Emmet replied. "Sixteen was… difficult."

They were silent a moment just staring at each other until Emmet cleared his throat. "So, are you ready for your jury Saturday?"

"I think so, yeah. Though as mum says you're never completely ready and that's okay."

"She definitely says that, so she does," Emmet answered. "Have you given any more thought to grad school?"

Trevor had brought it up at Christmas recess and had been met with encouragement but the more he thought about and researched it, the more school in America appealed to him. But the thought of leaving his family for a solid two years made his heart hurt. He didn't know how his dad had been able to leave Ireland for a midsized big city in the heartland of Middle America for three and a half years when Trevor was a child before Mara came back into their lives.

"I have but I'm not sure."

"Why's that?" Emmet asked.

"Well, for one it's expensive and two I don't know if I could be away from you all for that long."

"Don't worry about the money. Your mother left you that college fund and over the years I've been fortunate enough to add to it. You're set for grad school, if you want."

"It's not that, dad," he answered. "Not only."

"Being away from us?" he questioned.

Trevor nodded. "Yeah, I miss you guys so much right now and I'm only four hours away here."

"You've been away before. That time you went to stay with your Aunt Charlotte and Uncle Derek while your mum and I went on her comeback tour."

"I was twelve, it was an adventure," Trevor justified.

"Okay," Emmet chuckled. "Well, then the time you went travelling with your grandparents."

"I know but I had them with me. If I go to grad school in America, I'll be alone for two to three years."

Emmet was quiet for a long moment, but his eyes gave him away. "America?" His voice was tight.

Trevor clamped his mouth shut. He hadn't meant to let it slip.

"You're looking at grad schools in America?" Emmet clarified.

Taking a fortifying breath, Trevor plowed ahead.

"Yeah," he admitted. "I am. They're the best schools for

opera besides Italy, of course. And as a citizen, it's easier to get in. I haven't done anything," he hurried. "I've only looked."

Emmet cleared his throat softly. "Well, Trev if that's your desire, I back you. I'll miss you. But I back you. I would never want to stand in the way of your dreams."

"I know that. I just don't think I could be on my own that far away… never mind, you know what? My dad never taught me to be scared. He always taught me to follow my dreams and that's what I need to do."

A wide grin spread across Emmet's face. "That's my lad," he stated. "But now, tell me, any news on the other finals? How's studying going?"

Talking to his dad until well past one in the morning, Trevor signed off with a *talk soon* and *I love you.* Placing his phone on the nightstand, he pulled off his t-shirt and sweatpants. Flopping down onto the mattress in his boxers, he turned on the television and turned off the light.

Lying in the silver-blue light of the tele playing a repeat of an old Irish comedy, a face came to mind. Cassie. Cassandra Doyle, the most beautiful coloratura soprano he had ever heard and the prettiest girl in school. Not only pretty, but nice, genuinely nice. He missed talking to her, meeting her in the mess hall for lunch or walking home together from a late class. He always walked her to her residence when it was dark, just to be safe.

They were just friends and yet, they had kissed… once… but he did not think she knew it was him. Christmas, four months ago, the theater production department hosted a masquerade ball. They danced together. She asked his name, but he told her Phantom. Did she know it was him? He doubted it as he wore a variation of a red and black Venetian mask which covered his face from the top of his hairline down to just above his lip. It was one of his prize possessions from his Venetian trip with his grandparents.

He would never forget seeing Cassie when she arrived, alone. It was his chance. He had told her he was going home early so he could tell her how he felt about her. There was something fascinating and exhilarating about being a mystery to her. She gave him a task. One he could fulfill and bring to her without his mask so she would know who he was. Then he kissed her. Trevor flew to Norway and searched high and low for the bottle of perfume she loved. When he had found it, he felt like a king.

It made him want to punch the wall when he remembered Robbie McConaghy giving her a bag with the same colors as *his* mask with a bottle of her perfume. The memory of her confused face, haunted Trevor. When she hugged Robbie, clearly thinking the phantom was him, they met eyes and Robbie's smarmy grin forced Trevor's hand to clench.

Shaking out of his thoughts, Trevor turned on his side and stared at the show playing on the television. Soon, his eyes grew heavy and he drifted off to sleep dreaming of Cassie and their dance.

Chapter Three

Cassie looked over at Robbie's sleeping face as he lay on his stomach in her bed. They had been together since Christmas but somewhere in the back of her mind, she knew he was not the mysterious masked man she danced with and kissed at the Christmas ball. Her phantom. But he had given her the bottle of perfume she fell in love with when she backpacked through Norway and that was the task she gave her masked stranger but to this day, every time Robbie kissed her, she caught herself thinking of how his kiss was different. Robbie and the phantom were similar, they were both fit, tall, and had blue eyes, but Robbie's were never quite icy blue enough.

Shaking her head, she stood and pulled on her t-shirt. Heading to the small kitchenette, she poured some lukewarm coffee into her mug and taking the cup, walked over to the window to look out at Temple Road. Smiling as she took a sip, she remembered running into Trevor O'Quinn at the café the other day. She missed him. Not having seen him much since Christmas, she always enjoyed talking to him singing with him, being around him. Cassie and Trevor were in their final year of a music degree while Robbie, also a singer, focused on his acting future with a theater degree.

When Robbie showed up at the café with that insult, calling him a Yank, she nearly wanted to punch him herself. Robbie was not a kind person and though Cassie never thought of herself as violent, she had other reasons for wanting Robbie gone. Looking at the fading bruise on her left wrist, she covered it with her other hand.

Robbie swore the first time he hit her would be the last but every time she contradicted him, did something he didn't like, or refused to sleep with him, he would find a way to hurt her, always apologizing afterwards and she always accepted it. Not because she wanted to, but because she was afraid of what he would do to her if she didn't. That and his family had money… a lot of money and influence and wielded it like a weapon.

For the sake of her parents and five siblings it was best if she kept her mouth shut. Still the one good thing about the day was seeing Trevor. They had bonded over having American mothers and the love of music, a part of her hoped her masked stranger had been him but there was no way. He had told her he was going home before the ball and not attending.

Seeing him had brought back all the fantasies she had their first three years at Uni. His red hair, broad shoulders and light blue dancing eyes seemed to be something out of a romance novel, but he was real, oh was he real. Yet another reason she did not think her mysterious stranger was Robbie, his hair was darker than the red auburn she remembered.

Robbie's voice made her jump.

"Where are you?" He asked. She looked over at him to see him staring right at her.

"What do you mean? I'm right here," she answered.

"Physically yes, but mentally you were a million miles away," he said standing and walking to the small fridge to pull out a beer. Not pulling on his pants, he stood nude in her apartment. He had a nice physique, well-built and defined but he was a lot like his body, unforgiving, solid, and pretty but only on the outside.

"I was just thinking," she admitted.

"About what?" he shortened the space between them and stroked her cheek, ignoring her flinch.

"About my jury," she lied.

"You'll do great, love," he stated. "Just flash that brilliant smile of yours and you'll win them over." He smacked her arse playfully. But she wasn't amused.

"It takes a lot more than that," she replied. "It takes talent too."

"Well, yes but not always. Wear a skimpy outfit. I'm sure you'll pass with flying colors then."

"Are you saying I don't have any talent to pass on my own?" she asked, her temper getting the better of her. When she saw fire flash in his eyes, she looked down and away from him.

"You are very talented," he answered gripping her chin forcing her to look at him. "Just in many different areas." He kissed her hard, his hand causing her to simply take the bruising force. He pulled ack and looked down at her. "Don't forget who you belong to. I'll take care of you when you fail. I know who to talk to. But you need to make me want to help you."

She tamped down the immediate anger, betrayal, and disgust. Unsure why all the feelings she successfully banished when she realized who and what Robbie was, came back full force, she nodded once and looked over at her backpack.

"I have to get to class," she said.

"I'll see you tonight."

"I have a late training today."

"Since when?" He demanded drinking from the beer.

"It's a graduate student and the only time they can meet is at seven." She eased around him and pulled on her jeans and sandals.

"Who is it?"

Used to him demanding to know every aspect of her life, she answered with the name of one of the graduate students hopeful he wouldn't check up on her.

"How long will you be?"

"We have it scheduled until nine-thirty."

A small fib she hoped he wouldn't see through. So far, he had not caught on.

"What about dinner?" he complained.

"I was going to grab two sandwiches in the mess hall today at lunch and eat after my five o'clock class ends. Sorry."

"Fine," he huffed. "I'll see you in class tomorrow then."

"Yeah, great," she may have answered too enthusiastically but fortunately his male ego took it as she was excited to see him. "I'll see you then."

Knowing he would expect a kiss goodbye, she hurriedly

gave him a peck on the lips and left her room, not taking a moment to breathe until she was down the block.

Robbie was like a dark cloud hanging over her. *My own personal Robbie Raincloud.* She chuckled to herself. Before her desire to simply leave everything behind, the stress of school, singing, Robbie, everything, overtook her she headed to class.

After a hard workout in the gym, Trevor headed to the showers. He always enjoyed working out, his dad had taught him from a young age eating right and taking care of yourself were important, but not everything. Emmet always said *life is too short to be focused on physical appearance. Have that burger, eat that last slice of cake, but never take it too far.*

Trevor always wondered why his dad would say those things and when he was older, one day at a hotel pool in Brussels while on tour with Mara, he saw two scars on his father's chest. Roundish scars, almost like a bullet. Somewhere, in the back of his mind he had a faint memory of something, but it was merely flashes. Finally gathering enough courage, he had asked him. Emmet sat him down and told him the story of how he met Mara. He explained what happened with Trevor's grandparents, how they had custody over him, but his late mother had wanted Emmet to raise him even though Emmet never knew about him. He further explained the events at the County Kerry courthouse after he was granted custody and where Mara's crazy ex-boyfriend had shot him in an attempt to get back at Mara for ruining his life.

Since then, Emmet's *life's too short* speech made much more sense.

Trevor hummed as the water sluiced over his body and he lathered up the soap. His final was coming along nicely and was in five days, fourteen hours, and six minutes... not that he was counting. He had a lesson with a new graduate student early that next morning. He always took the early morning shifts. He did his best singing in the morning, a fact he attributed to his days as an altar boy at his family's church in County Kerry. His father rejoined the church when they returned to Ireland.

But the nervous energy coursing through him the last few days of classes, he forced himself to go to the gym. Class ended at seven, but it was already dark outside, and the gym was nearly empty, let alone the showers. He was alone. Which was why, when he heard a soprano voice singing Marguerite's final scene in *Faust*, he looked up, confused. Usually a duet, the female voice travelled through the tiled walls, the acoustics of the shower making her sound as if she was everywhere all at once.

Turning off the water, he grabbed his towel and wrapped it around his hips. Padding down the hallway careful not to slip with his wet feet on the tile, he followed the sound to the main hallway toward the door. Stopping dead in his tracks when he saw Cassie standing, her back to him, near the lockers. Her beautiful soprano voice filling the room. For a moment, he simply listened and watched her, but when she continued into the final song *Oui, C'est Moi J't'aime* and stopped singing to count the tenor's part, he could no longer resist. It had been far too long.

He began to sing.

Cassie gasped and turned around. Her eyes immediately going to his bare chest. Looking away, a blush crept up her cheeks.

When the tenor part finished, they stared at each other in silence and for a moment, he wasn't sure if she would continue, but something akin to fire flashed behind her eyes and, taking a step closer to him, she began again. They sang the rest of the aria together.

Chapter Four

The moment Cassie saw Trevor standing behind her, a white towel hanging low on his hips, she stared. Thoughts she never should have had entered her mind, and she felt her cheeks redden as she looked away.

His voice brought her attention back. They used to sing together all the time and she had missed him. The fact he was standing there, singing *Faust*, she took as a sign.

The tenor part finished, she knew at that moment, she could walk away, and nothing would change, or, she could continue, and they could sing once more together. The look in his eyes told her two things, one, he wasn't sure if she would and two, he was leaving the choice up to her.

Robbie's face flashed in her mind but so did the bruise on her wrist and the anger she felt. Locking eyes with Trevor, she took one step toward him and began singing again.

Trevor loved singing in any form; musicals, Irish ballads, jigs, pop songs, he even threw in a little American country as a nod to his birth mother's and his homeland, but opera... opera was his first love.

Maybe it was his stepmother's influence. Not an opera singer herself, Mara preferred lyrical ballads or musicals, but she was always singing and would always have all forms of music playing at their house. Both his parents and grandparents would take him to see operas and musicals on Broadway, West End or closer to home in Dublin. He had a well-rounded musical past, singing in church and school choir as well as gaining stage presence by being in local shows for musicals.

Singing an aria with Cassie was a dream come true. He'd sung in odder venues than the men's locker room. All too soon the song was over, and their voices bounced around the tile walls slowly fading.

Cassie smiled at him and he couldn't help but smile back.

"That was fun," she said.

He nodded. "I've missed you." Then, he caught himself. "Uh — I mean — I missed singing with you."

"I know what you meant."

They stood in awkward silence until the chill of the air made him shiver.

"You should probably get dressed," she said. "I'm sorry I interrupted your shower."

"I'm not," he replied. "But can I ask why you were singing in here?"

"I come here sometimes when it's late. The acoustics are amazing and normally there's no one here," she shrugged.

"I didn't realize how good they were," he said and again, he shivered. "Listen, I'm starving. Could I get you dinner?" At her hesitation, he continued. "Not like that, I know full well you have a boyfriend, but I need to eat, and I'd rather not do it alone. We can go to a pub on Grafton or that little café we met at the other day."

Again, her eyes dropped to his chest then back up. "Yeah, that'd be nice. Thank you."

"Great! Let me get dressed and I'll be right back."

She nodded and turned around as he raced back to the showers. Grabbing the clean clothes he was going to throw on, he was grateful he had packed a pair of jeans and a t-shirt that afternoon instead of his usual sweats. Once fully dressed, he met her at the door, and they walked to Grafton Street for a pint and a sandwich.

Cassie followed Trevor into the pub and grabbed a table while he ordered at the bar. Taking a moment to watch him, she couldn't help her mind drifting to him standing before her in nothing more than a towel. He was well-built, tall, over six feet, and broad shouldered. He was defined but not overly large, more of a soccer player, with lean muscles and strong legs. He had always been so very handsome in her opinion.

Seeing his auburn hair as it caught the light of one of the lamps, she bit her lower lip to prevent a self-incriminating groan escaping. As his hair dried, it had curled and lightened from the almost dark brown when wet, to the dark red it was in the light.

She caught herself wishing he had been her mysterious phantom who danced with her at the ball.

Cutting off her thoughts, he returned with two drinks and an extra-large sandwich. He smiled and sat. "I hope you don't mind; I got the rotisserie chicken sandwich."

"Not at all, looks great!" she said leaning forward.

"And it's Bulmer's *Pear* Cider still, right?" he asked indicating the bottle next to his Imperial Pint of Guinness.

Tears pricked the back of her eyes suddenly, knowing he remembered. Biting the inside of her cheek to stop the emotional response, she nodded. His brows furrowed for a second, but he said nothing and sat beside her, lifting one half of the sandwich onto the extra plate, and taking his glass of beer.

"Sláinte," he toasted.

"Sláinte," she replied.

They drank and ate in silence for a moment until he leaned back in his chair, half of his half of sandwich still on the plate.

"So," he began. "How have you been? I haven't really seen you since the session started."

She nodded and finished her bite before answering. "I've been good, yeah. How about you?"

"Murphy is running me ragged with his deep dive into theory," he answered.

"Oh, me too," she agreed.

"When do you have his class?"

"Wednesdays at three."

"I'm Monday," he said taking a long draw on his beer. "It's brutal. Eight in the morning."

"Ugh, I couldn't imagine," she leaned back taking her cider with her.

"It's okay though, you know? I mean, it's tough sure, but I've learned a lot."

"Me too. I'm just worried about the final. I don't know what to expect," she tapped her glass with her pointer finger, a habit she picked up as a kid.

"My grampa says to expect the unexpected and be pleasantly surprised," he said. "I'm planning on every eventuality."

"Will they be there? Your family. At the final?"

"They will, yeah," he answered. "My grandparents on my mother's side are flying into Dublin day after tomorrow. I have class then but my Uncle Innis, my dad's brother promised to go pick them up. We're all having dinner that night. Then my parents and all twenty-four of my cousins, and all six sets of aunts and uncles, along with my paternal grandparents and Great-Aunt will be there."

"You have twenty-four cousins?" she sputtered, shock evident in her tone and on her face.

He took a drink of his Guinness as he nodded. "My dad has three brothers and a sister along with his cousin who is basically like a sister to him and my mother's sister and my stepmum's sister. It's all very confusing. We O'Quinn's could have a dynasty," he chuckled.

"Wow... and I thought I was fancy with my eight cousins."

"Eight's a lot too."

"Not as many as twenty-four!"

Trevor chuckled. "My dad says he could divide us up and have a football match."

"Clearly," she laughed. He paused and she looked at him confused. "What?"

"Nothing... that's just the first time I've heard you laugh in a while."

She blinked and looked down, hiding the emotions that flitted across her face. He was dangerously close to flirting. With a sigh, he cleared his throat.

"How's Robbie?" he asked.

She looked up finally but shrugged. "He's fine," she answered.

"It seems pretty serious between you two, yeah?"

"I guess. Are you still dating what's-her-name?"

"Who?" he asked.

"Blonde?"

He grimaced. "Can you be a little more specific?"

She laughed outright. "Player."

He shrugged and took another drink. "I'm not currently dating anyone. I wanted to focus on my final year of school."

"I wish I had."

Trevor reached over and placed his hand on her wrist. Pain shot up her arm from the sprain Robbie caused. She flinched and pulled away, cradling her wrist. The horror on his face nearly broke her heart.

"It's not your fault," she assured. "I... hurt it. Tripped down the stairs at my residence."

"Did you get it looked at?" he asked.

She shook her head. "You need to. There could be damage."

"It's a sprain, nothing more. I promise. Thank you for caring," she said placing her other hand on his arm.

"Of course," he answered covering her hand lightly. "What are your plans for after graduation?"

"Not sure," she answered, grateful for the change of subject. "I was thinking about graduate school. You?"

"Same," he replied. "I was thinking America."

"Me too!" she smiled. "What schools have you applied to?"

"Ehm, none yet," he answered. "I have a decent college fund, thanks to my mom. When she passed away, she had most of her life insurance put into a fund for me. My grandfather and then my dad managed it and helped it grow. My dad's helped put money into it, too. But I don't know if I want to use it for grad school or if I want to keep it as a nest egg for my future."

"That's wonderful! I had to apply early for scholarship consideration. My parents are amazing, but they aren't well off and the farm drains them. I wouldn't have been able to study at Trinity if I hadn't gotten the full scholarship. But I'm hopeful a few of my top choices will pan out. They're on the East Coast so it wouldn't be too difficult to fly home once in a while."

"You wouldn't miss your family?"

"Oh, I would, but this is a chance of a lifetime."

"True," Trevor nodded. "I guess I just couldn't imagine leaving everyone behind for so long. Having grown up surrounded by all of them, it's been odd living on my own the last three years. But I have some family left in the States. In the Midwest. Indiana, actually. That's where I was born."

"I've never been, is it nice?"

"It is, yeah," he answered. "My mom was from there."

"I'm so sorry you lost her so young."

"So am I, but Mara, my stepmum is amazing. She definitely keeps my dad on his toes."

Cassie giggled. "Were those two people you were with yesterday your siblings?" she asked.

"Yeah, they were. Killian and Aoife. They're mum's and dad's kids. They're looking at Trinity for uni."

"That's so wonderful! I'm sorry I didn't get to meet them, properly," she said. "I remember my visits to universities. It was scary. I bet they like having you here."

"I always try to be there for them and for my younger cousins especially," he explained. His eyes darkened just a moment before he said. "But... my eldest male cousin; Lachlan, he's ten years older than me lost his wife and unborn child five years ago." Pulling out his phone, he huffed. "With everything going on, I completely forgot to call him on the five-year anniversary. I'm sure he was wrecked."

"When was it?" she asked.

"First of the month. I should call his cousin, Egan. I'm sure he was with him. He lives just outside of Dublin."

"You all seem close. I'm sure he understands."

"I hope so. No one should have to go through what he did."

"Can I ask... what happened?"

"Car accident."

"Oh, how terrible."

"It was. He was so young. Only twenty-eight, so was his wife. Now," he sighed. "I don't know. He's changed so much, of course. I try to always be there for him. Maybe one day he'll realize he's still alive. Ugh, let's change the subject. This is too sad for our reunion of sorts." She smiled and nodded. "Can I ask one other thing?" he asked.

"Sure."

"Why *Faust?*"

"What?" Of all the things he could have asked, she did not expect that.

"Tonight, when you were singing. Why did you pick *Faust?*"

She looked into her cider and smiled broadly. Not many people knew the answer to that question.

Looking back up at him, she began. "When I was a little girl, my mum was obsessed with *The Phantom of the Opera.* I think I have seen every single version of the musical or book-based movie. But there was one I remember vividly that shaped my love of the story. The musical is amazing but when I was old enough, about twelve, I read the book and fell so in love with it. Then my mum surprised me with a miniseries adaptation that was produced around the same times as the musical first started. It was about three hours long and focused on the book instead of the musical. Anyway, there's this scene at the end where Christine Daaé is singing to lure the Phantom out of the shadows. He shows up in his usual box and they begin to sing together. It's the final part of *Faust* and it was so beautiful that it made me fall in love with opera. Ever since then, I made it my mission to learn that piece so well it became my warmup, go-to piece if anyone asked me to sing. So... that's why."

Trevor nodded slowly. "The Phantom and Christine sang it together?"

"Yes," she replied. "It's somewhat the pinnacle of the movie. It's like the part in the musical of *Past the Point of No*

Return."

"Ah, that I do know. My mum and I always sang the theme song together when I was growing up. But I love that song."

"How sweet," she said. "I would like your mum I think."

"And she would love you," he answered. "Two diva sopranos, god help me."

"Awe!" she feigned indignation and smacked his arms gently. "Rude."

Trevor just grinned and laughed.

"Anyway," she went on. "It's the point in the story when Christine realizes she actually loves the Phantom and tries to save him."

Trevor nodded slowly; all trace of teasing gone. "So... in other words, I was your phantom?"

The saying, innocent enough, caused her to stare into the blue eyes across from her. The tenor of the voice saying the name was too high. That was one thing she couldn't get over. The phantom who danced with her had a deeper voice like Robbie's second tenor or baritone. But Trevor...

"Phantom?" she questioned.

"Of the Opera?" he offered.

"Oh, right," she agreed.

The corner of his mouth ticked up.

"What the hell are you doing here?" Robbie's voice demanded, causing her to whip around. He grabbed her wrist just as she saw the ugly look in his eyes. Pain shot up her arm as he tugged her to her feet.

"Ow, Robbie, stop. You're hurting me!"

Chapter Five

The second Trevor saw Robbie grab Cassie's wrist, he knew one thing was certain; she didn't get those bruises by tripping down the stairs. And that made his blood roar.

Pushing to his feet, he grabbed Robbie's upper arm.

"Let her go, you son of a bitch," he demanded.

"Go home, Yank, no one wants you here." Pushing Trevor away, he turned his eyes toward Cassie. "Class, huh? I knew you were cheating on me."

"It's not like that," tears formed in her eyes as she tried to pull away from him.

"Oh, it's not, huh? So, sharing dinner and drinks with

another man is just what? Being friendly?"

"We're friends," she justified. "Let me go!"

"Let her go," Trevor tried again, this time he didn't take no for an answer. Squeezing Robbie's shoulder with a punishing grip, he turned him around.

"Let go of me!" Robbie shouted. "I'll do what I want, bastard."

"I said," Trevor yanked Robbie around. "Let her go." Robbie did, but swung at Trevor catching his jaw. The pain wasn't nearly as bad as he expected but he wasn't about to allow it to go unanswered. Trevor returned the blow but hit lower to Robbie's solar plexus. The brute doubled over. Trevor grabbed the back of his neck and pulled him up. One more punch to the jaw and Robbie fell to the floor. Other patrons rushed in and held Trevor back while helping Robbie back up.

"I'm done, leave off," Trevor struggled against their grip.

"Please let them both go," Cassie begged.

"Do you know who my father is?" Robbie shouted. "I'll have you arrested."

"Arrest him and I'll stand witness for him. I saw you grab the girl and throw the first punch," one of the patrons holding Trevor stated.

"Aye, me too."

"And me." Other patrons agreed.

Robbie shrugged off their hands and looked pointedly at Cassie.

"Make your choice. Me? Or the Yank."

Cassie looked at Trevor then at Robbie. "I'm not choosing."

"You have to," Robbie forced.

"Leave her alone, you bastard," Trevor shouted.

"You would know, being a bastard yourself," Robbie spat back. "Your whore of a mother probably didn't know who the father was." Trevor struggled against the hold of the two men beside him. Unable to get away, Trevor watched as Robbie turned back to Cassie. "Choose."

"I choose myself, if I have to choose," she stated.

"That's not a choice," Robbie answered. "But it'll do for now." Straightening his shirt and wiping blood from his lip, he looked at Trevor. "I'll see you in jail." Again, Trevor struggled against those holding him back.

"Wait!" Cassie cried. "Robbie, wait. If I choose you, will you let Trevor go?"

"No, Cassie, don't," Trevor ordered.

"I won't see your life ruined," she replied not looking at him.

Robbie turned to her and a smug look crossed his features. "Yes, so long as you choose me."

Cassie closed her eyes for a moment then nodded and a rock settled in Trevor's stomach.

"Cassie, no."

"So be it," Robbie grabbed her again and tugged her out of the pub.

Trevor knew her tear stained face as she looked back at him would haunt him for the rest of his life.

Two days passed and everyday Trevor looked for Cassie everywhere on campus, even waiting around after his classes to see if he could find her. He hated not knowing what she was going through. He nearly texted and called her a few times but then worried if Robbie would see his attempts and hurt her. He knew nothing about her class schedule that session except she had theory with Murphy on Wednesday at three. Determined to see her, he waited outside the classroom in the hallway, skipping one of his lessons, but he was sure the old friend of his Grandma Dee would forgive him. The sweet eighty-year-old woman was a sucker for his dancing blue eyes and smile. He lost track of how many times she called him by his father's name. Answering to *Emmet* was better than the sore cheeks he got whenever she pinched his "cute dimples" as she called them.

Murphy's class began and Cassie wasn't there. Skipping classes that late in the year was definitely frowned upon, but knowing her as he did, she wouldn't skip class if she had a fever. Something wasn't right.

His phone chimed at an incoming text.

Uncle Innis: Heya lad, just wanted to let you know your gran and grandad landed safely. I've picked them up and we're heading home. Dinner is at six. They knew you were in class, so I promised I'd text you instead.

Trevor: Thanks, Uncle In. Don't tell Dad, but I skipped that class today. I'll tell you more later.

Uncle Innis: You better have a good reason for skipping so late in the year. But I can understand. Old Mrs. Bailey used to pinch my cheeks too. I'm scarred for life! See ya at six.

Trevor had to chuckle at that. Mrs. Bailey and his Grandma Dee had been friends for decades. All his uncles and his dad unwittingly rub their cheeks whenever he mentioned her.

When three-thirty rolled around, and still no sign of Cassie in the theory class, Trevor grabbed his bag and stalked out of the building heading toward the main road. He swore if Robbie McConaghy had hurt her, he would gladly face jail to get rid of him. Cassie deserved so much better. With that thought, he pushed into a different pub from the other day and sat at the bar.

Chapter Six

When it was time to leave for his six o'clock dinner, his mood was no better. Part of him wanted to keep drinking but he knew he couldn't do that to his aunt, uncle, and grandparents.

Settling his tab with the bartender, he walked to the bus stop to catch a ride to his uncle's. Innis used to have the flat directly on Grafton Street but after he married and they had Cait, with plans to have more children, he bought a house on the outskirts of town. Soon after, their son and two more daughters were born, and the studio apartment became a family rite of passage.

Every cousin who went to school in Dublin stayed there, rent free, and Trevor was the first to say how convenient it was.

The bus dropped him about half a mile from his uncle's and as he walked, he kept thinking of Cassie. If that bastard had laid a finger on her, he would be sorry. His mood darkened even more. As soon as the neighborhood came into view, he was tempted to just keep walking but, taking a deep breath, he forced the thoughts behind him and headed to his uncle's house.

He didn't even need to knock. The door burst open and his grandmother squealed.

"Hello, my darling!" she cried and threw her arms around him. He hugged her tightly, her familiar and comforting scent banished his dark mood.

Pulling back, she cupped his jaw and peppered his face with kisses. He chuckled and cried for mercy. One more hug and she let him inside. His grandfather stood in the entryway and embraced him tightly.

"Missed you, son," he said.

"Missed you too, grampa," he answered. "How was Spain?"

"Beautiful," he replied. "But come on in. Beer?"

"I'll take a water for now. I had a couple earlier," he admitted.

"Everything all right, sweetie?" his grandmother asked. "I mean, it's just you don't normally day-drink."

"You're right, gramma, I don't. There's a lot on my mind."

"Oh sweetie, wanna talk about it?" she asked.

"Not right now," he swung an arm around his grandmother's shoulders, pulled her into his side and kissed her temple.

"Surprise!" Voices shouted from the kitchen as soon as he rounded the corner. Trevor stopped in his tracks and looked around. Everyone was there. Every single one of his uncles and aunts, his other grandparents, his cousins – all twenty-four of them – even his aunt and uncle from America. Forty-five people were squeezed into the kitchen.

Trevor blinked but then a mile-wide grin spread across his lips.

"Hiya everyone," he said.

They all said hello and then laughed at the look on his face. Emmet greeted his son with a tight hug and a slap on his back.

"Damn, I've missed you, Trev," Emmet said.

"I've missed you too, dad," Trevor replied. "God, I really missed you."

Emmet pulled away to look deeply into his son's eyes. Trevor wasn't sure why, but he felt as if his father was reading his soul. Emmet smiled softly and cupped his jaw.

"Tell me later," he whispered.

Trevor breathed a laugh. He should have known his father would see something in his eyes. As soon as Emmet stepped back, Trevor was assaulted by hugs, kisses, thumps on the back, demands for piggyback rides from the younger cousins and give tastes of all the food cooking to make sure it was done or tasted good.

After everyone ate, some sitting, other standing and even some outside on a beautifully warm late spring day, the women urged the children outside to play and the men to go into town for a pint.

Knowing it was their way of telling everyone it was time for the ladies' gossip hour, the men agreed, kissed their wives, and filed out of the house. Trevor's mood significantly improved over the last couple hours and when the baker's dozen of them entered a pub off Fleet Street, four of them went to the bar to order and the rest slid into a corner booth. It was tight but they all managed to fit around the three tables pushed together in the corner with an L shaped booth lining the wall.

Cabhan, Sean, Lachlan, and his Uncle Derek from America carried the glasses of Guinness to the table to disperse among the men.

"Cheers, Cabh," Emmet said accepting his beer from his eldest brother.

Once everyone was served and seated, Trevor raised his glass in a toast.

"Thank you all for coming to support me this week, it's been an interesting final month of class but I'm so very thankful to you all for helping me."

"Always, son," Emmet winked and clinked his glass to Trevor's. "Sláinte."

"Sláinte," everyone toasted and then drank.

"Now, do you want to tell us what's going on?" Emmet asked.

Trevor sighed. "I honestly can't believe I'm that readable."

"To me, you are," Emmet stated.

"And me," his granddad, Orin replied. "Just like this one," he motioned to Emmet.

"And me, son," his grandfather, Curtis stated.

Trevor looked around the table. "Anyone else wanna comment?"

His cousins and brother just laughed.

"What's going on, lad?" His uncle Cabhan asked.

After heaving a sigh, Trevor leaned forward. "There's this girl..."

"I knew it," his Uncle Innis stated.

"Women," Peter, his American cousin shook his head. "What is it about them that makes us men all doolally?"

"Doolally?" his father, Derek asked. "That's... pretty accurate actually."

Peter shook his head and took a drink of his beer. "Where is April, Peter?" Trevor asked after his cousin's girlfriend.

"Oh, that's over. Been over for a while," Peter replied.

"Oh, mate, I'm sorry. I didn't know."

"Nah, it's all good, bro. But I'm planning on popping over to London to see Geoff after your jury. He's been nagging me to come over," Peter explained speaking of his best friend and military brother, Geoffrey Ainsley, Marquess of Garvey. They had met a year and a half ago when Lord Garvey, Lieutenant Commander in the United Kingdom Special Forces Reconnaissance Regiments, saved Peter's life when he had been a POW. Having been injured in the rescue, Geoff and Peter were sent to the military hospital in Germany. Their friendship blossomed but Trevor always wondered if it was more than that.

"I'm sure that'll be fun. Tell his *lordship* I say hey, would ya?" he teased knowing Peter hated it when Trevor made jokes about Geoff's blue blood.

"Will do, asshole," Peter answered with a wink. Trevor chuckled.

"Nice dodge, son, and not that I'm not interested in Peter's love life, or lack thereof—"

"Ah thanks, Uncle Em," Peter snorted.

"But you aren't going to get away from dropping a hint of *there's this girl* and getting out of our cross-examination," Emmet said. "What is it about her, son? Have you asked her on a date?"

"No," Trevor replied. "It's complicated."

"We're here," his grandfather Curtis said. "Talk to us. Between all of us here we have about four hundred years' experience with women."

"No, we have one-year experience four hundred times over because we keep making the same mistakes," Orin laughed slapping Curtis on the back.

Everyone chuckled but agreed and raised their beer in cheers.

"She's with someone else," Trevor admitted.

"Ah... Girl snatching, is it?" His Uncle Sean asked. "Better talk to your Uncle Innis on that one."

"Lay off," Innis teased. "Thank God I did steal her. You're happier with Ness."

"Can't deny that," Sean confirmed with a raised glass toward his brother.

"It's not like that," Trevor shook his head. "I respect relationship boundaries, it's just..."

"What son?" Emmet prompted.

"I better begin at the beginning. Her name is Cassie, Cassandra Doyle. We became friends our first year. Her mother is American, and we bonded over that and our love of music. Nothing happened. We were just friends. We dated other people, not a problem but we kept talking with each other and... I don't know when it happened, but I started comparing every woman up against her. Wanting the date to end so I could call her and tell her how disastrous it was. Wanting to hear her voice, wanting to see her every day, sing with her, be near her even if she didn't feel the same. It was strange and more than a little weird because I never felt that way before."

All the married men shared a look. His cousin Lachlan looked away and drank from his beer. For a moment Trevor wanted to stop for his sake. He had called Lachlan's cousin Egan to see how Lachlan was on the five-year anniversary. Egan simply sighed and told him two words; "not good." It seemed unfair to torture Lachlan with his woes.

"Lach," he started. Lachlan looked over at him, the same empty look in his eyes he always had for the last five years. "I'm sorry."

Lachlan shook his head and finished his beer. "I'm going to get a refill. Go ahead. I doubt I'll have much to offer in the way of advice." The bitterness in his tone nearly gutted Trevor. They hadn't talked yet since the anniversary. Knowing Lachlan wasn't petty enough to be angry at him, he still felt the guilt for not being there.

Lachlan stood and took his glass and his father's. Cabhan put a hand on his son's forearm but dropped it when Lachlan locked eyes with him and shook his head ever so slightly. As Lachlan walked toward the bar, everyone at the table stopped.

"I shouldn't have brought it up," Emmet said. "I'm sorry, Cabh."

Cabhan leaned forward and smiled slightly at his brother. "He's going through hell. But that doesn't mean the rest of the world stops. He knows this, that's why he removed himself. He knows his limitations. It's all right, go on."

Trevor hesitated and his eyes trailed to Lachlan standing at the bar. He had received his pint and was slowly drinking while watching the game on the television. His body language gave off leisure but the way his back rose and fell on heavy breaths, coupled with the large shot of whiskey the bartender placed before him and he tossed back like water, it was clear he would rather be left alone. Trevor took a second to watch him. Even at just thirty-three, Lachlan's dark brown hair was greying at the temples and some sprinkled throughout, his toffee colored eyes were heavy and empty. He was a very handsome man, but he looked so much older.

"Go on, son," Cabhan encouraged.

"I fell in love with her. But I had a rival. Robbie McConaghy. His father owns the McConaghy Whiskey. He wanted her too. Last Christmas the drama and music department put together a Masquerade Ball for all the students to kick off the Christmas Holiday and celebrate the end of the school session. Not to be confused with the Trinity Ball in April. I thought, here's my chance to see how she feels without her knowing it was me. I told her I was going home early and not attending but I did, wearing the mask I bought in Venice," he nodded to his grandfather who was there with him when he purchased the souvenir. "She didn't know it was me. We danced and I told her I cared about her but didn't say who I was. She asked me to tell her, but I said give me a quest. Something she wanted for Christmas that no one else could or would get her. She requested a bottle of her favorite perfume she could only get in Norway. I promised I would get it for her and present it to her unmasked for her to know it was me. We sealed the agreement with a kiss and god, I didn't want it to end. She was everything I ever dreamed of and it's not from lack of experience. I had never had a kiss as intoxicating as hers. That next day, I got on a flight to Norway—"

"Wait a minute, what?" Emmet questioned.

Trevor winced. "I didn't tell you, I'm sorry."

Emmet sighed. "You're twenty-three, you can do as you please but it's not safe to leave the country and not tell anyone."

"I know, I'm sorry." Emmet huffed but nodded. "I found the perfume and got back to campus. I had wrapped it up in the red, black and gold colors of my mask and was walking across the green to give it to her when I saw Robbie talking to her near the Holy Well and giving her a bag with the same colors. I watched in disbelief as she opened it and low and behold it was the perfume."

"Shite," his uncle Innis muttered.

Trevor nodded. "How he had heard of our code, I'm not sure but she believed him, and they've been dating ever since."

"You didn't tell her?" Peter asked.

"No, how could I? There are unspoken rules about that sort of thing. I'd have looked whiney and desperate. But that part, though it bothers me, isn't what boils my blood."

He looked up as Lachlan came back over and gave his father his beer. Sitting, he said nothing, only listened.

"What does then?" his cousin, Oisín asked.

"I'm pretty sure he abuses her, hits her," Trevor revealed.

The men went silent and the unspoken anger filled the area. Tension built and Trevor was halfway to believing they would all get up and head outside tracking Robbie down like some old mafia movie. Looking at each face in turn, they all looked ready to defend Cassie and kill the bastard. Oisín, the largest of them all, even at twenty, and who was his Uncle Cabhan's youngest child, stood. Though Oisín had a humorous side, he could be serious when he wanted to be and at that moment, standing at the corner of the table, braced between Uncle Tom and Uncle Cabhan, he pulled himself up to his full height nearly six and a half feet. Taking

53

a deep breath, he puffed out his muscles which bulged and corded beneath his Iron Maiden band t-shirt and looked ready to maim.

"Sit down, Colossus," his father teased. "We're all angry at that boy, but we need to talk. How do you know he hurts her?"

"Because I saw the bruises on her wrist and... we went to the pub the other night together as friends," Trevor explained what happened when Robbie showed up and after, how he hadn't seen her since.

"Have you gone to the cops?" Peter asked.

Trevor looked over at him seeing the determination in his cousin's eyes.

"How can I? His father owns a third of Ireland."

"If you are sure he's abusing her, you need to do something, son," Curtis said.

"But I don't want you involved in this. Not with him. He could be dangerous," Emmet spoke up, his hand unconsciously going to one of the bullet wounds on his chest and rubbing it as if a phantom pain hit him. "Go to the police by all means, but don't let him get to you."

"I know you don't want me to get involved because of what happened to you with mum's ex, but Dad, he doesn't have a gun. He's just a bully. A rich bully."

"I don't care if he doesn't have a gun and you don't know that for a certain. I need you to be careful," Emmet stated.

"There's nothing I can do anyway," Trevor replied.

"Bollocks," more than one man said.

"You need to make sure she's all right," Cabhan replied. "But I agree with your father. You need to be careful."

"Do you have her number? You could call her," Peter offered.

"What if he's taken it?" Trevor asked. "I've already thought of that."

"When's her final jury?" Orin asked.

"Oh, good idea," Curtis replied. "You could go to that."

"It's Sunday, after mine," he answered.

"I hate to say this," his Uncle Derek spoke up. "But if she honestly didn't know it was you behind that mask after three years of friendship and allowed that jackass to trick her... speak to the police by all means but, is she worth it?"

Trevor looked his uncle straight in the eye, not offended or angry by his words but wanting him to know how serious he was.

"Yes, she is."

The others leaned back and nodded. "Then," his father began. "What do you want to do?"

"I don't know."

"Do you know where she lives?" His Uncle Tom asked.

Trevor shook his head. "She moved last year and when we studied, we used to meet up on campus. I don't know maybe I am overreacting."

"If you care about this girl and she's being hurt you should do something," Orin stated.

"But maybe Uncle Derek's right."

"Whoa, what?" Emmet questioned.

"Well, maybe I'm over thinking it and if she can't be

bothered to know me then what's the point?"

"I'm only going to say this once and you better listen," Lachlan began. Everyone went silent. "If this girl means anything to you and I mean *anything* then it is your duty to protect her. She may not know what she's going through. She may turn a blind eye to it. She may think she's trapped. But whatever it is, you have to give her a way out. You cannot sit there and tell me you love her when you sit on your arse and do nothing to save her."

Trevor swallowed audibly at his cousin's impassioned words, knowing how difficult it was for him to say them. Trevor nodded.

"I do love her," he said. "And even if she doesn't feel the same for me, maybe it's time for her to know she has a way out. And if not, then at least I have done what I can."

"Find her," Lachlan went on. "Don't wait for something irreversible to happen. Trust me you will always blame yourself if you don't at least try to save her." Cabhan placed a hand on his son's forearm as he spoke. Lachlan looked over at his father and took a deep breath. Then looked back at Trevor. "Trust me."

Trevor nodded. He would go to her jury. It was only four days away, he could wait... he hoped.

Chapter Seven

The day of Trevor's jury final arrived faster than he anticipated. Classes kept him busy and working on his surprise for the final gave him little time to think about Cassie, but she was still the first and last thing he thought about during the day.

Saturday, he arrived at the recital hall early, after choking down a quick light breakfast. He wasn't nervous to sing, he loved it, it was more not knowing what to expect. He was confident the faculty was not expecting what he had planned but would they like it or not was one of his biggest concerns.

The free tickets were all give out and his family alone could fill nearly half of the one hundred and five seat auditorium.

Walking up to the stage, he saw the usual black grand

piano and the music stand. With no one else around, the entire area was lit, and the house was in the dark. He sat down on the bend and tinkered with the keys. Playing a piece, soon his mind drifted to Cassie and he played the notes of *Faust's Oui C'est Moi J't'aime,* humming as he played. The memory of her flushed face when she turned around to see him standing behind her. The memory of her beautiful voice ringing off the tile rose goosebumps on his skin. Her beautiful light brown hair and light eyes was a combination he never admitted he was attracted to. Blondes were usually his preferred type but there was something about Cassie's ash brown and blue that made his jaw tick. He missed her but he wanted her, and he couldn't have her. That was the most painful thing.

The main door opened, and he looked up.

"Hello?" he called, unable to see who had arrived.

"Sorry, sweetie, I didn't mean to interrupt you," his stepmother's voice drifted to the stage.

"Mum," he smiled and stood. She walked up the steps to the stage. He hugged her tightly, taking in her perfume remembering when the mix of her fresh sea breeze mixed with his father's fern and pine had helped him sleep as a boy. "What are you doing here?"

"Well, I texted you, but your phone was off. I figured you were rehearsing."

"I was, sorry. I always turn my phone off so not to be distracted."

"I know, sweetheart," she grinned. "Where do you think you learned it? But I wanted to see if you needed any help warming up or wanted to go over anything."

"That'd be grand," he replied. "I was just about to start but wanted to play a little, get my mind off things."

"It's nerve-wracking, I know," she pushed his hair off his forehead. "But you'll do great."

"It's not just about singing."

"Oh?" she asked.

"Did dad tell you?"

"Your father and I promised long ago that if our kids tell us something in confidence, so long as it doesn't hurt you, we will keep it to ourselves so you all know you can trust us."

"It's not confidential," he shrugged. "But I guess I didn't say he could tell you, but I didn't say he couldn't either."

"What is it, love? Is it a girl?"

Trevor chuckled and sat back on the bench. "Why am I not surprised?"

Mara smiled and leaned against the edge of the piano. "Talk to me honey. You may not look at me as a woman since I'm your mum, but I am one," she winked. "I'll be happy to talk to you about a woman's mind."

"It's a dangerous thing."

"Tiss," she smacked his arm affectionately. "You've been hanging out with your father and uncles too much."

Trevor laughed. "Can't deny it. And honestly, mum why are women so difficult to understand?"

Mara thought a moment. "We can be but sometimes that's normally because we don't know what we want. Sometimes we don't know what is best. Other times, it's because men just don't understand what we want and that frustrates us. Or they leave dishes in the sink after I've washed them, or they don't put away the laundry when I've left it out for him or he forgets the hoover and leave it out for days claiming he didn't see it."

"Are we still talking about me? Or should I duck and cover until dad gets here?" Trevor questioned.

Mara chuckled. "Sorry, off topic. But we women love our men. I have loved your da' since I was eight years old. We have disappointed each other, hurt each other more than you'll ever know, love, but marriage, commitment is not easy. It's an uphill battle everyday but with the right one by your side? It's so worth it. And I wouldn't give you, Killian, and Aiofe or Emmet up for anything. He is truly the love of my life and if I can help you understand a woman, her wants and needs then maybe I can help you have the kind of love I have with your father. Emmet is everything to me. Always has been. I long for each of my children to tell me they found their one. I want you all to be as fulfilled as I am."

"I'm starting to think we need to change the subject before you reveal something about yours and dad's sex life."

She laughed. "Well, I wouldn't dare, but I will say it's as satisfying now as it was when we were in our thirties."

"Okay, definitely TMI," he waved her off.

Mara giggled but looked at her stepson with all the love of a biological mother. Trevor felt that love deep in his soul and smiled back at her. "I love you, sweetie, and if I can help you find the love of your life, I would be so happy."

"I love you too, mum," he said. "And I just want *her* to be happy. With me or not, I only want her to be happy."

Mara gasped slightly then gazed at him. "She means that much to you."

"Aye, she does," he answered.

"Do I know her?"

Trevor shook his head. "But I would like you to meet her

one day."

"Tell me all about her and then we'll warm you up for your big performance."

"Thank you, mum," he said. "For everything."

Mara kissed his cheek and took a seat next to him as he began telling her all about his angel of music.

"I won't be home for a couple hours," Robbie said as he pulled on his jacket. "You know how these dinners are."

Cassie nodded and watched as he grabbed his keys. "And you know how mum and da' are. Until we're married, you aren't welcome."

The thought of marriage caused bile to flood her mouth, but Cassie swallowed it down and keep her face devoid of reaction.

"Be careful," she called.

"I will," he answered. "Watch something on the tele. I won't be long."

"Take of your time," she said. "I'll be okay."

Cassie waited until the door closed behind Robbie. She was never invited to dinner with his parents and hadn't even met them. That suited her just fine. There was somewhere else she would rather be and a quick glance at the clock confirmed she was already late, but she pulled off the sweatpants she wore over her black hose. Finding the little black dress she had stashed away earlier that week, she pulled it on and zipped the back as fast as she could.

Her makeup already done by order of Robbie to cover the

fading bruise on her cheek and handprint on her neck, she grabbed her purse and high heels. Pulling on her trainers, she raced across town to campus.

Chapter Eight

Robbie pulled up to his parent's house, though house seemed like too small a word. The place was positively palatial. Sitting on acres of land, the sprawling complex was his home. Though there needed to be love to make it a home and *love* wasn't something in surplus supply with the McConaghy family.

Glancing at the time, he cringed. It was two minutes past seven and his mother always demanded punctuality. Though she was never physically nor truly verbally abusive, her disappointment would be difficult to avoid. Most of the time, it was a look or even a quip that always made his brother and him wonder who she was directing her words to when speaking her mind.

Not wanting to waste more time, he put his car in park

behind his brother's Land Rover and pulled out his suit jacket from the hanger in the backseat. Making sure his tie was straight, he rushed to the door. He pulled the chain and heard the bell ring throughout the house. The door took so long to open he fidgeted with his phone before eventually hearing the solid oak creak.

"Good evening, Master Robert," the old butler said with a bow. "Your parents and brother are expecting you."

"Of course, they are, Kelly," he stated. "That is why I'm here. And they're clearly waiting for me so be so kind as to step aside so I can make up some of the time it took for you to shuffle over and open the door."

"My apologies, sir," Kelly bowed again. "They are in the study lounge, sir."

Kelly moved to one side and Robbie didn't wait for the old man to show him the way. The clock laughed at him showing ten past the top of the hour. Hurrying to the study lounge door, he opened it and came face to face with his family.

"Good evening. My apologies for being late," he said. "That fool of a butler took so long in answering the door, I thought I had gotten the date wrong."

He nodded to his brother seated on the settee, a glass of whiskey in his hand and his father in his usual wingback chair before the fire. Walking toward his mother, a woman of just gone fifty though she would never admit it and with more plastic in her body than lined the oceanic coasts. Still, she looked elegantly beautiful with her blonde dyed hair and her silver silk evening gown. Her white wine in the crystal stemware rested on the mantle as her long French tipped fingers delicately held her cigarette holder between her fingers.

"Robert, dear, we nearly quite gave up on you," her clipped English accent gated on his ears. The woman was from Wicklow, Ireland but thought an English accent would make her appear more polished.

"No indeed, mother. I was delayed by two minutes by traffic getting out of the city. Some concert or other at Vicar Street," he admitted kissing her on the cheek.

"Still, you should have planned for that," she said returning the kiss in a very French way of never actually touching his skin.

"It's only ten minutes past, lad, no harm done," his father said.

"No of course not, if one does not mind waiting," his mother replied.

"I do apologize, mother," he said stiffly.

Finally, Kelly appeared at the door and poured Robbie a glass of whiskey, offering it to him on the silver platter he had grown up with. His mother seemed perpetually stuck in the turn of the century. The wait staff wore livery to serve at table and Kelly always had his white gloves on hand. It was like he had stepped into some BBC period drama.

Taking the whiskey, he turned to his brother, older by two years. They were never very close but as they were set to inherit their father's distillery fifty-fifty, he always tried to keep the lines of communication open.

"How are things, Charles?" he knew better than to call his brother *Charlie* in front of their mother.

"Things are fine," he answered.

"I thought I saw Elise in Grafton the other day," he said speaking of his brother's fiancée.

"Very possibly," Charles replied. "She was shopping for the honeymoon."

"So, all is set for September then?"

"Yes, father has given me time off from the distillery and the announcement has been in all the papers."

"I still do not know why she insisted on taking a professional photograph like an engagement announcement in jeans and a t-shirt. We are not to be known as common," their mother said bitingly.

"I believe it was her mother's idea, mother," Charles replied. "Something about wanting it to show us as more approachable. Besides her friend made those shirts for us." The shirts in question were black with white lettering showing Mr. & Mrs. at the top, then their name in the middle followed by the date of the wedding. The shoot was outside Elise's parent's home near a stone bridge. Both Charles and Elise were smiling laughingly. Robbie thought it would have been a good photograph, had it not been his eldest brother and heir to their mother's ideology.

"More approachable," she tsked. "Unsuitable. I've said it before. I will say it again, you should be marrying someone more like us, dear. Someone who will not embarrass us."

A muscle in Charles' jaw ticked as he clenched his teeth.

"Come now, love," their father spoke up. "We come from nothing and I don't intend to forget it."

"You have always made that clear, dear," she spat. "But the truth is we are better. We have a status we must maintain. At least I have not failed with Robert. He will never bring someone unsuitable home. Will you, dear?"

"I will attempt not never to embarrass you, mother." Though the thought of Cassie's farmer family did give him pause.

"There now, you see?" she said.

Charles' face grew red and his hand clenched around the

glass as he steamed. Their father walked over to him and placed a calming hand on his shoulder. Robbie watched as they shared a moment. Charlie had always been sensitive and unable to withstand their mother's rebukes as much as he could. Their father always could calm him.

In that one moment, Robbie felt more alone than ever before. He had never understood his father. Never understood how he could allow their mother to speak to him the way she did. He sometimes wondered why his father had married his mother. It wasn't as if they loved each other. Mother treated him more like a possession than a husband.

But on the other hand, he could understand. His father was an embarrassment. He was weak allowing a woman to dictate his life. Robbie shook his head. He would never allow it in his life. No woman would rule him.

"At least," his mother continued. "When and if you do find someone, Robert dear, be sure, if she isn't of our society, you can at least control her. And you know of course sometimes that means more honey than vinegar. But always have control over her. Unlike your father and brother, of course."

Charles and their father took a deep breath as one, just as the gong was struck.

"Ah," she beamed. "Dinner. Come now."

She swept out of the room and Robbie followed but still caught the hushed whispers of his father and brother and stayed close by the door.

"Damn her. Damn that woman to hell," Charles hissed.

"Charlie, she still is your mother," their father spoke low.

"I don't give a damn what she is. She has no right to speak to you, me, or about my fiancée like that. I love Elise and I don't care one iota if Mother thinks she's unsuitable. She's suitable to me. I love her. Doesn't that matter?"

"Of course it does, son," their father said. "But you have to understand your mother. She is always looking for a way to better herself and us along with it. She's lost herself somewhere along the way."

"Maybe all that plastic surgery has addled her brain."

"Charlie," their father warned gently.

"I'm sorry, but you should not let her speak to you like that, da'. It sets a bad precedent."

"You and I both know what would happen if I said anything. Not yet at least," their father answered.

"How much longer? How much more of this can you take? I see what is has done to you in the past," Charlie sounded concerned.

"Things have already been set in motion, son. I give it to the First Monday in August. She will be out of our lives and we can live how we want."

"You can't imagine she'll go quietly," Charlie said.

"No, of course not and I'm sure Robbie will want to go with her. Do you think you could run it without him?"

"He'll want his cut, of that I have no doubt," Charlie bit. "But yes."

Robbie's fist clenched as he listened at the door. They were planning on disinheriting him.

"There's a clause in our marriage contract. As soon as my heir and a spare have graduated university I can do as I please. That is why I've lived like this. But don't worry. My solicitor is on standby with the papers. And she cannot contest them. It will be over soon. As soon as Robbie graduates. Trust me, son."

"I do, da'," Charlie sighed. "I just hate that Elise has to put up with her bullying. I can handle me but she's sensitive."

"I know, son. I'm only too sorry for it. Come now. Let's go and not a word of this to your mother."

"Never. My loyalty is to you, da', always."

"I love you and Robbie so much, lad. But I see a strain of your mother in him and it scares me."

"I see it too."

Robbie stood frozen by the door in the shadows as he watched his brother and father leave the room. He couldn't bring himself to tell his mother, she was exceedingly difficult to live with, but he could not believe his father had taken his brother into his confidence and not him. Maybe his mother was right. Maybe he needed to think about using more honey than vinegar in more than one relationship. He liked to be in control. He had a temper, but was it his fault he was raised to be like that? No, of course not. He was always good at manipulating emotion. He'd have to do it again. He wanted stability. He'd reveal he knew his father's plan at the right time. The time *he* chose. He'd have his father and brother where they deserved. Controlled by him. Now, to get Cassie. He knew she was pulling away, her date with the Yank was enough indication. So how to get her where he could control her...

Become like him. Like Trevor. Shouldn't be too hard and as long as he never lost sight of his true goal, he could always manipulate her feelings just so. That would work. He grinned as he sauntered into the dining room, making sure to lock eyes with his father and brother, making them squirm with concern he had overheard. A plan for his family and girlfriend already forming. He'd still be his usual self to his mother, he couldn't afford for her to get suspicious, but another person would need to be created to keep Cassie. Someone different.

Someone like the Yank.

Chapter

Nine

Trevor had sung ten songs from his repertoire ranging from opera to pub songs. As he looked out to the nearly full auditorium, he saw the judges at their long table about two-thirds of the way back, their little clip on lamp illuminating his score sheet. They kept their faces stony, but he couldn't help seeing the slight raise of their eyebrows when he belted out the high note on *Una Furtiva Lacrima.*

After playing one of Chopin's nocturnes on the piano for his instrumental component, he had reached the end of his set. That was when the judges could throw anything at him, but he had one more thing to do.

His surprise.

Nodding to his accompanist, the man took his seat at the piano and waited.

"I wanted to take a moment to thank everyone who came out to support me today, your time could have been spent doing anything else but I thank you for your generosity in sharing this memorable night with me. Before I end my portion of the evening, I wanted to do a little something different. If I could have the house lights lifted a bit, please?" Trevor asked the light booth operator. Once he could see everyone, he continued. "I don't know if you've noticed, but I love to sing." The audience chuckled. "But what I love more is to be surprised. So, with the help and support of my accompanist, I want to turn this over to you all. I need seven people to please think of a song, any song, you would like me to sing and I will put them all in a medley, chosen by you and made up on the spot. Surprise me." At the confused murmurs of the audience, he went on. "I want to assure everyone there are no plants in the audience. In fact, Professor Murphy, sir, would you be willing to assist me?"

His theory professor looked at him for a moment, then finally nodded. "Could you assure the audience, sir you know nothing of what is happening?" Professor Murphy agreed and Trevor continued. "Please, Professor, choose seven people at random and they will tell me their song choices." The professor reluctantly agreed and stood. "Thank you, sir. Now if you have a song in mind, please put your hand up."

The professor picked seven people including Emmet who winked at his son and called out *Raglan Road,* his stepmother's favorite song and a song that meant a lot to both his parents. Trevor chuckled but agreed. There was everything from *Man of La Mancha* to *Wild Mountain Thyme* to even more modern and classic pop songs. After the seven were chosen, Trevor turned to his accompanist, fortunately they were all songs the pianist knew and with the indulgence of the audience, Trevor waited until the graduate piano student had worked out the transition not playing a single not so it would be a surprise to Trevor.

"All right," Trevor turned back to the audience. "I appreciate you all being here tonight. After this, it will be time for the professors to quiz me. You are all welcome to stay, but if you would prefer to leave, we will have a ten-minute break after this medley. Once again, thank you all."

With a nod to his accompanist, he began to sing the medley in the order it was requested, no music, nothing written down, simply a test of his musical knowledge, memory, ability, and creativity. He was happy to say, at the end of the medley, he sang each of the songs in order. Thanking the audience once more, he turned to his pianist and shook his hand.

Some students got ready to go as the audience gave him a standing ovation but when the applause died down, a voice from the crowd shocked him.

"Mr. O'Quinn, sing one more song. An encore if you would."

Trevor turned back to the audience, but the house lights had dimmed again.

"Who said that?" He asked.

Movement to his right drew his attention, the woman was still in darkness, but he could make out the shape.

"Sing one more song," she said again.

The house lights lifted once more, only slightly and he saw her.

"Cassie?" he breathed. She looked beautiful and he was relieved to see her well. But he couldn't help but see the extra makeup on her face. His eyes went down to her wrist where her arms hung by her sides. The bruise had faded into a light yellow. She raised an eyebrow when he looked back at her. Clearing his throat, he spoke again.

"What would you have me sing?"

"*The Phantom of the Opera*," she said.

"Which song from the musical?"

"The main theme," she replied.

"That's a duet," he answered teasingly. It was amazing how much lighter he felt seeing her there. They fell back into an easy rhythm of non-flirtatious flirtation.

"So it is," she replied.

"Do you happen to know a soprano who knows the piece?" Trevor asked.

The students who were getting ready to leave, stopped, and sat back down.

"I just might," she answered.

"Then please, have her join me. It's a tenor's dream to sing the part of the phantom, though... I have no mask with me."

Her brows furrowed for a moment. He kept giving her messages, but he was sure she never understood the deeper meaning.

As she joined him on stage, he nodded to the accompanist who, a wide grin on his face, moved to the portable organ on the other side of the stage.

"I beg your indulgence once more, but I can never deny a pretty woman." With a wink, Trevor had the audience enraptured again. He dared not look at his family. Most, if not all of them knew who she was to him.

A pause of absolute silence followed and then, those first few powerful notes from the organ resounded in the small space of the recital hall.

Singing Christine Daaé had always been Cassie's dream but to sing it opposite Trevor was unforgettable. Memories of their duet in the locker room flashed in her mind but as much as she loved singing *Faust* with him, she needed to hear him as her phantom. A niggling suspicion kept tickling the back of her mind. His constant use of *her phantom* or *having a mask* made her wonder. Was Trevor indeed her mysterious masked stranger from the Christmas Masquerade?

Suppressing the chills that ran up her spine as he stalked behind her, commanding her to sing as she hit high not after high note at the end, she should have been worried or scared he would hurt her like Robbie. But something reflected deep in his icy blue eyes, told her he never would hurt her. As her last high note rang out through the auditorium, they locked eyes and slowly she leaned toward him. His eyes darted down to her lips. She licked them instinctually. His eyes flared and his pupils dilated. He wanted to kiss her just as much as she did.

She felt his breath tickle the fine hairs on her face and tease her lips and then, the audience erupted in cheers. She jumped and Trevor flinched. Pulling away as fast as they could, they faced the audience.

Trevor was her friend. He never said anything about wanting more than that and she respected his choice. Not to mention she wasn't free. As much as she hated Robbie's temper there were so many good times with him too. She decided she had been so caught up with the character she was inclined to look at him that way. She ignored the fact his eyes dilated.

Shaking out of her thoughts, she faced the audience, smiled, and bowed. The standing ovation lasted a couple minutes and even the theater director stood and applauded.

Shyly looking over at Trevor, she smiled at him and headed off the stage. He started to go after her but stopped and waited back on stage addressing the audience once more.

Cassie rushed out the door and into the night. The cool air caressed her skin, calming the fire that had spread from the pit of her belly to every inch of her body. There was something about Trevor O'Quinn. Something about singing with him. Something about being around him, talking to him, laughing with him. There was just something about him that made her skin too tight, her body too hot and her mind too cloudy.

Dear god... she wanted him.

Wallowing in her recent discovery of wanting a man she claimed as a best friend all while dating someone else, she didn't hear the theater director behind her until he tapped her shoulder. Nearly jumping out of her skin, she turned to see the horror filled look on his face.

"Sorry, Professor Lipscomb," she apologized. "I didn't hear you."

"That's all right, Miss Doyle. I apologize I didn't announce myself," he said.

"No, no, my fault really," she forced a smile. "Can I help you?"

"I was hoping you would come back inside. I wanted to speak with you and Mr. O'Quinn together for a moment."

Cassie always appreciated how Professor Lipscomb took the time to learn everyone's last name that studied in the fine arts college when most professors called them by *you* or nothing at all.

"Oh, um, I appreciate it, but I can't. I'm sorry," she stated seeing some of the other students and audience members leave.

"Oh, please," he nearly begged. "I must speak with both of

you urgently."

She bit her lip and looked behind her, why, she didn't know. But she half expected Robbie to jump out of the bushes and grab her.

"How much longer?" she asked.

"Well, thanks to his impromptu medley, it takes one of the large components out. He only has to sight read and he's finished. Please, come back in. It won't be long. I promise."

Cassie thought for a second. Unsure why the theater director would want to speak to them. She checked her phone for the time. Robbie wouldn't be back for another hour. Her curiosity peaked, she nodded and walked back into the recital hall with him. The thought of seeing Trevor again after she just realized she cared about him as more than a friend, made her stomach flip and her palms sweat.

Chapter Ten

Seeing Cassie race out of the auditorium and not going after her was one of the hardest things Trevor had done. But seeing her come back in, was even worse.

Knowing the judges still had their part of the jury to do, he had to clear his mind, or he would never concentrate enough to pass the recital.

Scanning the audience, he found his family. Most of them were chatting with each other during the ten-minute break, but his father's eyes were staring directly at him, not paying attention to the others around him. Trevor took the strength he offered and filled his lungs to capacity, holding it for a long moment, then letting it out slowly. His breathing technique taught by his mother's best friend and singing partner Colm, helped him calm down and focus his mind. No woman was worth throwing away the years he spent in college nor the grade he was hopeful to receive for the recital.

When the corner of Emmet's lip ticked up and he winked, Trevor knew, with his family supporting him, he was ready to tackle anything the judges threw at him. Cassie sat in the empty chair near the back on the aisle and Professor Lipscomb the theater professor, slid his way through the row to his seat. Soon, the judges drew Trevor's full attention.

"Mr. O'Quinn, due to your very unconventional and surprising use of your free time, we only have one thing left for you," Professor Murphy said. His voice giving nothing away.

For a split second, sheer and utter panic hit Trevor squarely in the gut and he felt like throwing up what little of the lunch he had. Did they hate it? He was trying for surprise but unconventional? *Shite,* he thought, but then he stopped. That was their way of throwing him off balance. Focusing back, he forced the queasy feeling down and listened.

"We need you to go two things, sight read a theory piece and perform it. Have you ever heard *Savitri* by Holst?"

Trevor swallowed self-consciously. Holst was never kind to his singers, but he thought for a long moment, he had to make sure. The whole point of sight reading was for it to be a piece he had never heard.

"Not to my knowledge," he answered.

Trevor waited as his composition professor handed him the sheet music. He tried not to let the various vocal runs worry him but the three minutes he had to study the piece went by quickly.

One more steadying breath, a glance at his parents who smiled encouragingly to him, and he was singing.

He wasn't sure why, but the piece was one of the hardest he had ever performed. Afterwards, he could not read the judges as they thanked him for his time and began writing. It was customary for the judges to give out the grades after some deliberation. The audience was dismissed with Trevor's thanks and his family promised to wait for him outside.

As the professors deliberated, Trevor saw the theater director, Professor Lipscomb get up and walk over to Cassie still sitting in the audience. He spoke to her quietly for a moment, then they both headed his way.

The hair on the back of his neck stood on end. Lipscomb smiled warmly at him.

"Mr. O'Quinn, excellent job," he praised.

"Thank you, Professor."

Trevor breathed a little easier. "I wanted to speak with you and Miss Doyle because I have a proposition." Neither Trevor nor Cassie spoke. "The theater department as you know, every year puts on a production in tandem with the music and dance departments. This year we were toying with a couple ideas, but we finally narrowed it down. We were going to make an announcement Monday but after seeing both of your performances, I must say I am very happy to tell you first and offer you the lead roles."

"I'm sorry, sir," Trevor started. "Lead roles in what?"

"Oh, forgive me, I get ahead of myself sometimes. Ever since the Christmas Masquerade Ball we have all decided this year's musical production is to be *The Phantom of the Opera* and I just found my Phantom and Christine."

Trevor stared at the theater director. He heard his words, but his mind failed to process them. Something he didn't tell Cassie earlier was, he had always longed to play the part. Ever since he was a young boy. It was the first musical Mara and Emmet took him to see.

"What do you say?" Lipscomb asked.

"Excuse me," Cassie said softly and rushed out of the auditorium.

"Uh — Miss Doyle?" Lipscomb called after her. But when it was clear she would not stop, he turned back to Trevor. "What do you say, Mr. O'Quinn? Do I have my Phantom?"

Phantom? Cassie wanted to scream. And with her as Christine? She nearly hyperventilated. But how the hell could she possibly say yes when Trevor would be the Phantom?

If one thing from singing together at his jury proved anything, it was that she could not be around Trevor O'Quinn. He was like a fire, a magnet, a siren. There was no way she could. Robbie would kill her. If anything, he would hurt her more than before. Her dream was staring her in the face, and she had to walk away. Trevor deserved it. He deserved to be the star. Dear god, how she wished she could say yes... to a lot of things, but there was no way she could possibly do anything.

Tears rained down her cheeks and she tried to stop the pain blooming in her chest until she was safely tucked away in her apartment. As soon as the door shut behind her, she let a sob escape.

"Where have you been?" Robbie demanded coming out of the bathroom. Another sob escaped when she saw him.

"Robbie, please," she begged. His face changed and she couldn't help but stare. He looked... concerned.

"Babe, what's wrong?" he asked softly coming over to her.

He crouched down and pushed the hair away from her face. She expected him to pull it and force her look up at him, but he didn't. His touch was gentle.

It was moments like that she saw why she initially cared for him, but the memories of all the times he hurt her prevented any sweet feelings.

"Talk to me, Cassie," he said. "What happened?"

She looked at him and finally spoke. Did you know they're planning on doing *Phantom of the Opera* this year?"

His brows furrowed. "Who is?"

"Trinity, they're putting it on as the collaboration end of year production."

"Really?" he questioned. "That's a big production. But why are you crying?"

"It's my dream role."

"Ah, baby. I'm sorry. You're crying because you have no chance at getting it?"

Her brows furrowed. "No," she spat. "I'm crying because they offered me the part and I want to take it, but I can't."

"Really? Huh... why can't you take it? Do you not feel up to it? It's a challenge."

"No, because of who they want to play the Phantom."

"Well," he chuckled. "Isn't it obvious? I mean, we'll have to tone it down a bit so they don't know we're dating but I think, with some help, you'd do a good job and we'd be great. I'll put in a good word for you."

"What are you talking about?"

"When they give me the role of the Phantom. I know a few

teachers who wouldn't mind taking you on as a favor to me. They're expensive but I can cover it for you."

Cassie's blood ran cold. She stood slowly, unable to hold herself back.

"They're not going to offer you the role of Phantom. They already offered it to Trevor."

"Who?"

"Trevor O'Quinn," she answered.

"The Yank?" he questioned.

"Yes," she spat. "He's playing Phantom. Not you."

Robbie stared at her for a second then laughed. "Not for long."

"No, Robbie," she answered. For some reason, a strength unlike any other surged through her. "He *is* playing Phantom and I don't care what you say, I *am* playing Christine Daaé. It's my dream role and I have already been offered the part. You can audition for whatever two-bit part they have left, but one thing is for certain, until the show, I don't want to see you. I don't care what you threaten to do to me. I don't want to see you. Get out. Now!"

He stared at her for a long moment, until he finally scoffed. "You won't last long without me."

"I'm willing to take that chance. Get. Out."

He grabbed his coat. "We're not done. I'll let you cool down, but you'll come begging for me to take you back and I don't honestly know if I will. But fine. I'll see you in rehearsal. I hope you can live up to their expectations. I have my doubts."

He slammed the door when he left, rattling the picture frames on the wall. She grabbed the one of her family before it fell off. Gazing into her parent's faces, she cried fresh tears. They had always supported her but since she started dating Robbie, he had forced her to lose contact with them. Over the last five months, she had stopped calling and their calls went unanswered. They didn't even know she was singing tomorrow for her final jury. She itched to call them but knowing it would only make her cry more and then she would have a hard time singing the next day, she refused. Instead, she looked around her room trying to see one place untainted by Robbie.

He was everywhere. She couldn't stay there, she had to leave. Packing a quick bag, she left the flat and found her way to Grafton Street. Before she could find a place to stay that was in her price range, she had to find Trevor and apologize for running out like that.

She remembered he stayed in a small studio apartment above one of the stores, but she didn't remember if it was a pub, a deli, or a chipy. She walked up and down the street looking for the right one.

Finally, she saw the one landmark she remembered, a bust of Oscar Wilde. That was the building and he was flat number three.

Hurrying up the stairs, she found number three and knocked. No answer.

Checking the time, she realized he was probably still out with his family celebrating. She had no doubt he passed with flying colors. Still, she wouldn't be able to sleep without talking to him. She sat with her back to the front of the door, set her little bag beside her and leaned her head back. Before she lost the nerve, she opened her email app on her tablet and sent an email to Professor Lipscomb apologizing for her hasty departure and accepting the role of Christine in *The Phantom of the Opera*.

Her eyes burned and slowly, she closed them, leaned her

head back against the door and fell asleep.

Dammit! Robbie wanted to scream, but his mother's pristine voice rattled around his head. *We do not scream. It is undignified.*

Robbie hated it but he plastered a look of mild contentment on his face, unsure if anyone would be taking pictures and walked to his apartment.

That wasn't how it was supposed to go. The Yank had put a wrench in his plans, and he wasn't sure how to fix it. Cassie had never stood up to him like that. Clearly, Trevor had influenced her, and Robbie would have to break their friendship once and for all. But it was easier said than done. The Yank may still have the mask, he could still tell Cassie he was the mysterious man she met at the masquerade. Robbie couldn't let that happen.

But how?

Cassie was his and no one else could have her.

Unlocking his flat, he walked in and looked around. Compared to Cassie's hole of a place, his looked like a castle. His servant came out to greet him, took his coat, and took his order to pour him a large whiskey. Once he was along, he took a deep breath, holding his cut tumbler of whiskey and sat in his armchair. What could he do? His idea of becoming like the Yank didn't seem to work. He was not a delicate imp like the bastard, but he would have to. He needed to let her run over him like the Yank allowed. He needed to dig deep for his nonexistent emotions and bring them to the surface. His mother would never approve. But then again, she wasn't going to be in the picture for much longer if his father had his way.

Downing the whiskey, he closed his eyes and planned. His

emotions wouldn't surface but fake ones... well, he was an actor, wasn't he? Testing it out... tears filled his eyes on cue, and he grinned.

It was time to perform.

Chapter Eleven

Seeing Cassie run out of the auditorium again tore at Trevor. But he could do nothing. Turning back to Professor Lipscomb, he heard him ask;

"What do you say, Mr. O'Quinn? Do I have my Phantom?"

"Professor, I would be honored," he said.

"Oh good," he gushed. "Now to get Miss Doyle convinced."

Trevor said nothing only smiled slightly. "Thank you, sir."

"No, thank *you* for such a marvelous final. I have no doubt of the outcome."

"Mr. O'Quinn," Professor Murphy called from the table.

Lipscomb smiled once more and left the stage. "We first wanted to say that your little stunt about picking seven people at random to make you sing a medley was degrading, demoralizing, demeaning, and downright debasing."

Trevor's stomach pitched.

"But that is because I hate picking anything at random. It is not in my nature and I find it abhorrent to try and make it random. Other than that... it was bloody brilliant." At the professor's slight smirk, Trevor let out a breath and nearly felt lightheaded. "Your preemptive strike on the jury was unexpected, exhilarating, and fun... for some," his voice teased. "The reason we allow our students to do anything in the first place is to see how you react to the freedom. You, like many others could sing songs, play the instrument, or pick pieces that do not challenge you. You did none of those. You broke the mold. You, Mr. O'Quinn surprised us, and we are not usually surprised. Your ability to open to the audience without knowing what they would say, either makes you entirely foolish, or completely brilliant. Since you performed so well, we all agree it is the later. Congratulations, Mr. O'Quinn, you not only passed, you will be exceedingly hard to beat. We look forward to seeing your future endeavors and look forward to guiding you in *Phantom*. You gave him the title role, Eric?" he asked Lipscomb. At his nod, all the professors smiled. "Good. Thank you, for such a rewarding evening, Trevor."

Trevor beamed. "Thank you, all. I deeply appreciate you indulging me. I had a good time trying to come up with something different and I have to say I am pleased with my performance tonight."

"As well you should be," his aural skills professor said with a smile.

"Thank you. Thank you all. It has been extremely rewarding to learn from you. You each contributed to my development as a musician and actor. I could not have done this without you."

"It was our pleasure. You are free to go and be sure to celebrate your success."

"I will send an email out to you as soon as the rest of the cast is set with the rehearsal schedule, Mr. O'Quinn. See you the week after graduation!" Mr. Lipscomb called.

"Thank you, sir," he bowed and after embracing his friend and accompanist, he headed down the steps, up the aisle and out the door. Tugging at his bowtie and top two buttons as he went.

His family all gathered near each other outside. They turned as one to look at him. He schooled his features, deciding to play with them a little.

"Well," he said dejectedly. "Do you want the good news or the bad news first?"

Emmet and Mara exchanged a look then turned back to their son.

"Bad," Emmet stated.

"The bad news is, I have to stay a little longer on campus after graduation in a week."

"What? Why?" Emmet asked.

"And the good news?" Mara questioned taking her husband's hand in hers.

"The good news is, not only did I pass with flying colors, but they offered me the role of Phantom in the University's production of *The Phantom of the Opera* opening mid-July."

Everyone shrieked with happiness and rushed to him. Engulfed in a big group hug, Trevor laughed and hugged them all, reveling in such a weight being lifted. Now, if only he could get Cassie away from Robbie and standing at his side as his Christine, and better yet, as his girlfriend, his world would be complete.

"This calls for celebration," Emmet said. "Dinner res is," he checked his watch. "Now. Let's go." Slinging his arm around Trevor's shoulders, his father pulled him in tightly and kissed his temple. "So damn proud of you, son."

Trevor beamed at his father's words and together they walked the two minutes to the restaurant Emmet had reserved.

After dinner, the celebration with his family lasted well into the evening and wee hours of the morning. Trevor said goodnight, promising brunch tomorrow at his family's hotel; St. Helen's off the N11 across from Innis' neighborhood. They all piled into taxis and he headed in the opposite direction to his flat in Grafton Street. He wanted one more beer, just to continue the enjoyable feeling of the buzz he had, but decided to get home, crawl into bed, and watch a show he enjoyed or read.

Fumbling with his keys, Grafton Street was still bustling with people out on a Saturday night, but his cozy bed was calling him. He took the steps two at a time and turned the corner of the hallway. Stopping dead in his tracks, he blinked his eyes to clear the slight haze from the beer and to make sure he was seeing correctly. Cassie sat outside his flat, fast asleep, curled up on her side using her little overnight bag as a pillow.

Chapter Twelve

Cassie was dreaming about a handsome redheaded knight carrying her off to his castle and making sweet, passionate love to her. But she could never see his face. Every time she tried, it was blurry, and she could never focus enough to remove the invisible mask.

He had just pulled her into his arms and whispered her name when she opened her eyes and looked into the non-blurry face of Trevor O'Quinn. His eyes were a little glassy and hooded as if he had one too many at the pub, but he smiled softly at her.

"Hey," he said. "What are you doing here?"

Looking around, she realized she was in the hallway of his flat and not in some beautiful castle. Then, her mind caught up with her and she realized where she was and why.

"Trevor," she hummed and smiled. "I'm sorry. I needed to see you and when you didn't answer your door, I knew you were probably out celebrating with your family. I just sat down to wait and must have fallen asleep."

"Can't say I'm used to arriving at my flat to see a beautiful woman waiting for me," he teased.

He had called her beautiful and pretty in the past, but after her realization that night of wanting him, she felt her cheeks redden.

"You know, you could have called or texted me. I would have been happy to tell you where we were. You could have joined us," he went on.

"I didn't want to intrude," she answered. "You were with your family." At the final word, she couldn't hold back her tears. A sob burst forth and hot, ugly tears soon followed.

Trevor knelt before her and gently pulled her to him. Cuddling her into his chest, he simply held her as all the pain, fear, and anger of the past few months overflowed. She sobbed against his white dress shirt.

All the while, she latched on to his voice and the vibration in his chest as he hummed a song and rubbed slow sweet circles on her back. It grounded her. With his help, the tears subsided, and she pulled back to look up into his light blue, slightly bloodshot eyes.

Why couldn't it have been you? Why did my masked stranger have to be Robbie? If indeed it wasn't Robbie as she suspected, why had she wasted five months of her life on him, when she could have been with Trevor?

"I kicked Robbie out," she finally said. Trevor said and did nothing. "I wasted so many months on him and he did nothing but hurt me, mentally and physically. I told him about *The Phantom,* and he thought, he honestly thought, he would be cast, and I didn't have a chance at Christine. He never believed in me. Not like you have."

Trevor smiled softly. "Is that why you're sitting in my hallway?" he asked teasingly.

"Heh," she breathed. "No, I wanted to thank you for always encouraging me and tell you I'm sorry I ran out on you and Lipscomb earlier. It was all just too much."

"That's okay, but I would really like you to say *yes* to Lipscomb."

"I already have," she admitted. His eyes grew wide as a grin broke across his lips.

"Really?"

She nodded. "I sent him an email before I fell asleep." Pulling out her tablet, she checked her emails and a giddy feeling stirred in her chest. "See?" she turned the tablet around for him to read Libscomb's reply email saying how pleased he was.

"Well, looks like you're going to get your wish," Trevor said. "You get to be Christine."

"Opposite you," she replied.

"Opposite me," he agreed.

They stared at each other for a long moment, not saying anything until Trevor broke eye contact and stood, offering his hand to help her up.

"Yeah, I should get going," she said softly, gathering her things.

"Can I ask why you have an overnight back if you kicked *him* out?" Trevor asked.

92

"He's everywhere at my flat. I can't get away from him there. Honestly, I want to burn the whole place and start over."

"Where are you staying tonight?"

"I'm not sure. I don't have a lot of money, so I was probably going to school and sleep in the women's locker room."

"You can stay here," he offered.

"Oh, no," she shook her head. "I couldn't put you out." Her cheeks instantly flushed.

"You're not. You take my bed. I have a couch. It's fine, really," he moved to unlock his door and took her bag for her. "Please, stay here. That way I know you're safe."

"The women's locker room has a lock."

"Cassie, who knows what Robbie will do, now you've kicked him out. I would feel better if I could be there to protect you."

She stared at him, one hundred and one scenarios racing through her mind but finally, her body exhausted, she agreed and walked into Trevor's flat.

Chapter Thirteen

Cassie was there. In his flat. His eyes scanned the visible area to make sure he hadn't left a random pair of underwear out. He was happy to say, in his state of insomnia the night before where worry for the final prevented him from sleeping, he had cleaned the entire four hundred square foot studio. The only thing out of place was the plate with his remaining half of toast from that morning's breakfast.

"You can have the bed. I'll take the couch. Bathroom is through there. If you give me two minutes, you can have it all to yourself," he was fair near bursting after the beer and water at the pub.

She nodded and he set the bag down on the bed, hurrying to the bathroom. After finishing and then brushing his teeth, he emerged from the small room to find Cassie in the kitchen washing his breakfast plate.

"Sorry," she said looking up at him. "I had to keep busy and this was the only thing I could think of to do. It's really clean. I saved your toast though." She offered it on a paper napkin as if it was a piece of gold.

"Thank you," he smiled. "But you didn't have to. That was from breakfast and I should have tossed it earlier."

She smiled but her stomach growled. Blushing, she looked away. "Sorry, I haven't eaten anything today."

Trevor headed to the kitchen and opened the fridge. "Do you eat eggs?"

She nodded; brows furrowed. Then, seeing what he was doing, she tried to stop him. "Oh, Trevor, no, you don't have to do that."

"I know I don't have to," he turned and winked. "But I want to. Sit down, wherever. It won't take long."

She didn't argue and sat on the barstool, he used as a breakfast nook. She watched him chopping onions, peppers, and ham as the pan warmed. Once the food was chopped, he pulled out two blocks of cheese and a grater. She said nothing as he drizzled olive oil and sautéed the veggies. He hadn't made his scrambled eggs for a woman in over a year. His last girlfriend was a vegan and before her, he never really had a woman stay over at his flat. The studio was his sanctuary, not many people were allowed in.

It didn't take long for the vegetables to sauté and the eggs to cook. Laying strips of Asiago and White Cheddar cheese on top, he quickly plated the food so the cheese would not over melt. Turning back to Cassie she was staring at him, but soon her eyes moved to the food on the plates in his hands. He liked a woman with a healthy appetite. He never appreciated the women who ordered the smallest thing on the menu while he ordered a burger. That was something he never had to worry about with Cassie. Anytime they went to the cafeteria together, they always seemed to get the same thing.

When he set the plate down in front of her, she ravenously attacked the eggs, barely taking a breath between bites.

"This is so good!" she finally exclaimed taking another bite.

"I'm glad you like it," he answered. "Eggs were the first thing I learned to cook. It's come in handy a few times. Especially when traveling. My mum said she wouldn't have to worry about me starving if I could make eggs."

Cassie giggled. "I burn my eggs."

"Oh no," Trevor laughed.

"Yeah, it's bad... gourmet I am not."

"I could teach you," he offered. "Don't let it be said Trevor O'Quinn sat on his arse when there was a lady in need."

Again, she giggled, and it was music to his ears. They fell silent again and soon the eggs were gone, and Cassie yawned.

"What time is your final tomorrow?" he finally asked.

"Same time as yours was today. Six."

"Good then you can sleep," he said. "My family asked me to brunch at their hotel tomorrow. Would you like to join me?"

"Oh, I don't want to intrude."

"You wouldn't be," he said. "Besides, if you don't fill the day, you will wallow and panic, trust me. And that's not you."

"You're right," she agreed.

"Is your family coming down?" he asked.

Her eyes lowered to the empty plate, tears gathering in her eyes as she shook her head.

"I'm sorry, Cassie," he said softly and took her hand in his. "Could they not make it?"

Again, she shook her head. "They don't know about it."

Trevor tried not to react and kept his voice light. "Why?"

"I haven't talked to them for a little while. Just haven't told them."

"I'm sorry."

"Stop apologizing for god's sake," she spat. "It's not your fault. It's mine. Robbie didn't... he didn't want me to talk to them. He didn't like that they are farmers. He didn't think he should fraternize with *those sorts of people*. He made me feel horrible every time I talked to them. So, I sort of, just stopped."

Trevor nodded, a plan forming in his mind. He had her brother; Padraig's number from a while ago and would be calling him first thing tomorrow.

"Hey, don't think any more about that tonight. You need to rest," he stood and pulled a blanket off the end of the bed and a pillow. "I'm on the couch. Take the bed."

"No, that's not fair to you."

"I don't mind, really."

"But the couch is too small for you."

She was right. The couch was not made for someone over six feet tall to lay out comfortably, but there was no way he was letting her take the couch. "I'm good, Cassie. Really."

She bit her lower lip, still seated at the barstool. Her eyes drifted to the full-sized bed in the corner. "I wouldn't mind sharing the bed with you. I trust you."

Unconsciously, Trevor swallowed hard, but nodded slowly. "If you're sure."

"I am." Cassie slid off the barstool and went to her bag, pulling out an oversized t-shirt and a small pouch. She smiled slightly and headed to the bathroom.

For a moment, he stared at the closed door and tried to calm the raging blood coursing through him. Yes, he was a player, some would say *like father like son*, but he also would say, like his father, he never took advantage of the situation, nor a woman. But at that moment, he had to tell his body to calm down.

Turning back to his dresser, he searched for a pair of pajama bottoms and a comfortable t-shirt. Usually one to wear only his boxers to bed, if anything at all, it would be different to wear a shirt. Fully dressed when she opened the door, he tried not to notice her nervously clasped hands in front of her, nor her cute pink-painted, chipped toenails as her bare feet pressed together. The oversized t-shirt she wore came to midthigh and covered the important parts. His eyes trailed up to her face. It was devoid of makeup and for the first time, he saw the true bruises. The entire left side of her face was a yellowish purple and the handprint around her throat had faded, but he could still make out all five finger marks.

Anger flared through him. How could anyone do that? How could a man hurt a woman, any woman? The anger flooded through him so fast it made him lightheaded.

"Bastard," he muttered.

She swallowed audibly. "I'm sorry. I thought about leaving the make up on, but I didn't want to ruin your sheets."

"No, it's fine. It just makes me angry at him. How could he do that to you? Why did you stay with him?"

"I thought I didn't have a choice."

"You always have a choice."

She shook her head. "I was stunned the first time, but he was drunk, and he kept apologizing for it. I forgave him. And the second time and the third until I just expected it." She clenched her fist at her side and looked away. Trevor crossed the room in three strides.

"Don't," he said. "Don't turn away from me." She looked up at him and he saw the pain she had been hiding. "Never turn away from me," he whispered.

Cassie's emotions overcame her. She leaned forward, pressing her body against his. Tilting her head up, she invited him to lower his lips to hers. He was tempted. Dear god, was he tempted. But he took a step back, his hands gently on her shoulders to make sure she didn't fall.

"It's not that I don't want to, Cas," he said when he saw the confused look in her eyes. "But I'm tipsy and you're..."

"Emotional?" she offered.

"Aye," he breathed. "And I want to be completely sober when I kiss you again."

"Again?" she questioned.

Shite. He held his breath. He hadn't meant to say that.

"What I mean is," he blinked hard. "I've dreamt of kissing you and when that happens, I want to be fully cognizant of it."

She smiled softly. "You're right, me too. I'm sorry. I wanted to feel good and forget. But Robbie and I only had the fight today, you don't deserve to be a rebound. Thank you."

"Don't thank me," he chuckled. "I would be happy to kiss you if I wasn't tipsy." They were quiet for a long time but soon, she wrapped her arms around his waist and laid her cheek against his white t-shirt, holding on. Her high messy bun of light brown curly hair tickled his nose and he tried not to think about how well she fit in his arms.

"Come on," he coaxed. "I'm exhausted. Let's get you to bed."

She nodded, then pulled away suddenly. "I'm so sorry," she gasped. He was instantly on alert. "I didn't ask, how did you do on your jury?"

He breathed easier and grinned as he remembered. "Passed with flying colors," he announced.

"That's amazing!" She cried and hugged him tighter. "I had no doubt whatsoever! You so deserve that. I'm so happy for you!"

"Thank you," he said. "I look forward to celebrating with you tomorrow when my *angel of music* passes her final too."

She bit her lip and Trevor tried not to focus on the movement.

"I hope so."

"Hey, you will. I know you will. You are amazing."

Tears welled in her eyes again, but he gently wiped them away with his thumb. "No more tears. Come on," he led her to the bed. She crawled in under the sheets and moved to the far side of the mattress. Trevor sat and swung his legs up, tucking the sheets around him. Cassie curled up on the edge of the bed, her back to him.

"That's not comfortable for you," he stated. "Come here."

She turned and looked at him. He opened his left arm to her. She hesitated but eventually nodded and scooted closer to him. Placing her head on his chest, he wrapped his arm around her and took a deep breath.

"Thank you," she whispered.

He smiled against her hair and reached beside him to turn off the lamp. Once bathed in complete darkness, he kissed her hair and laid his cheek against the top of her head.

"Sleep." He said softly before closing his eyes and drifting off to a deep, dreamless sleep.

Chapter Fourteen

Cassie slowly woke to the smell of freshly brewed coffee and the soft sound of a man humming *Music of the Night* from the *Phantom of the Opera.* Not just any man… Trevor.

Opening her eyes, she lay on her side facing the kitchen. Trevor's back was to her and she took a second to observe how the white t-shirt pulled tightly across his back and how his light blue polka dot pajama pants hung low on his hips and sculpted arse. For a man in his early twenties, Trevor had an impressive physique. His height and red hair almost made him look like a Viking Invader of old and she had to catch herself fantasizing about him whisking her off to his ship and carrying her far away from there.

Trevor turned before she had a chance to cover her

obvious ogling. Her eyes trailed up to his face where a knowing smirk tipped up the corner of his mouth. Her face heated and she looked away.

"Good morning," he said.

"Hi," she answered. Her throat was a little raw and her face and head felt thick and heavy from all the crying he had done the night before. She cleared her throat and tamped down the fear that churned inside her belly. Her jury was in, she checked the clock, eight hours and her throat was nearly raw.

Trevor carried two mugs over to her.

"Here," he said. "This might help. My mum swears by it."

He offered her one of the mugs and held the other. His, she could smell was black coffee, but that could dry a singer out. Turning to look at hers, she sniffed. A bit of honey, a bit of lemon. She took a sip... and warm water.

"Mmm," she hummed and closed her eyes. The ache in her throat soothed almost instantly. "Thanks."

"My pleasure," he replied. "Did you sleep all right?"

"I did, yeah," she answered. "Probably one of the best night's sleep I've had in a while."

The corner of his mouth ticked up and she wished she knew what he was thinking. But the look was gone before she could read more into it.

"Now," he patted her knee. "Let's eat. I'm starving."

For a moment, she forgot about his family and brunch. She stood excitedly, then realized he was supposed to meet them. Turning away, she spoke softly.

"Sorry, you should go to your family. I'll be all right. I don't think I could eat anything anyway."

"Hey, where did you just go on me?" he asked gently taking her shoulders and making her look at him.

She shrugged. "I don't know. Never really met family before, I guess."

"You mean, you've never met Robbie's family?"

She shook her head. "They're odd like that."

"Well, it's fine, I've already texted my dad. They're looking forward to meeting you. You can't not come now. Come on. I'd really like for you to join me."

Debating, she finally agreed. It would be a new experience for her.

"Give me twenty minutes?" she asked.

"Sure," he agreed. "We need to leave in thirty."

She nodded and paused. "Can I use your shower?"

"Of course," he replied. "It's a little tricky, let me get it started and show you."

Once showered, dressed and bruises successfully hidden, she didn't want to have that conversation with Trevor's family, she opened the door without thinking and came face to face with Trevor's bare chest as he pulled on a dress shirt.

"Sorry," he said and turned around. "I thought I'd be done by the time you got out, but I was distracted by Lipscomb's email."

Turning his back didn't help since he only had on a pair of light blue cotton boxer briefs that hugged every part of him to mid-thigh. She caught herself staring at his round arse covered in the thin material.

She snapped her attention away and cleared her throat. She needed to get a handle on her hormones, it's not like she hadn't seen a man dress before. She had also seen Trevor only wearing a white towel. But standing in his flat after sleeping in his bed, with her head on his chest, made it all so much more... intimate.

"No, that's okay, sorry I forgot for a second," she said looking away. "I should have called out to you."

"I'm glad," he answered. "It means you're comfortable."

He grabbed his jeans and pulled them on, tucking in his shirt and looping his brown belt around his waist. She looked down at her jeans and the peasant top she had grabbed before she left.

"Am I too underdressed?" she asked.

"You kidding? You look great!" he replied.

"Are you sure? I think I still have my black heels in my bag from yesterday. I could wear those."

"If you want," he answered pulling on his cognac colored dress shoes.

He stood from the bed, looking delicious. Cassie scolded herself again and looked away.

"Are you okay?" he asked.

She nodded. "Sorry."

"It's okay. Let's go if you're ready."

"I am," grabbing her small bag and purse, she dug for her high heels. Nearly crying eureka when she found them. The right heel could really dress up an outfit. She pulled them on and followed Trevor to the door. He locked it and they walked together to the bus stop.

"Do you have a car?" she blurted out. Wishing she could pull the words back and choke on them. She didn't want him to think she thought less of him if he didn't.

"About five," he answered. Her steps faltered and he chuckled when he caught her arm. "My dad used to own a car dealer in Killarney. I have one on campus, but I hardly drive it since I can get everywhere by bus or cab and Dublin traffic sucks!" he laughed. "I have it parked in long term student parking and only really use it when I drive home."

"Sorry, I didn't mean to sound ungrateful."

"No, no worries," he gave her the side smile she loved so much. "If you want, we can take it. Or a cab."

"No, it's okay," she answered. "The bus drops us right at the door of the hotel. I just can't walk far in these. They look cute but they hurt."

"I'm sorry I didn't think."

"It's fine, really," she answered as the bus pulled up and they got in."

Chapter Fifteen

The bus ride to the hotel was longer than Trevor anticipated but that was partly because he kept thinking of the night before.

He had woken once during the night to feel her head on his chest, hand possessively holding his side and her legs intertwined with his. She moaned when he moved slightly to get a better look at her sleeping face. The bruises made him angry at Robbie but did nothing to change how beautiful she was to him.

He was so caught up in how adorable she looked hopping from one foot to the next pulling on her high heels, he didn't even think about his car and it was both a good and bad thing. Good, because he wasn't sure he would be able to be that close to her in such a confined space for any length of time and focus on driving.

Bad, because he didn't think about her having to walk in those heels. However sexy they made her long legs look, they could not be comfortable. But as he sat beside her thinking about everything that transpired between them in the last twenty-four hours, his phone chirped a text message.

Pulling his phone out of his back pocket, he checked the message. A reply from Cassie's brother who he had called earlier that morning while Cassie was still asleep.

Padraig: Spoke to mum and da'. Da' can't make it on this short of notice due to the last of the ewes being born, but mum and I are on the road. We'll be there by four.

Trevor: That is wonderful news! Here's my address. You and your mom are welcome to stop off there first and meet me. I'm planning on going to her final too. We can go together.

Padraig: Will do! Thank you for reaching out. Mum was so happy you did. I'm looking forward to catching a pint with you and mom is excited to meet you.

Trevor: Same here, mate. We'll get a pint after dinner. My treat.

Padraig thanked him and signed off.

"Everything all right?" Cassie's voice startled him. He pocketed his phone and looked over at her.

"Aye, why?"

"You have a weird smile on your face."

"Oh," he instantly changed the smile and took her hand. "Just looking forward to having breakfast with you and hearing you sing tonight."

"Ugh, don't remind me," she answered. "Will you help me warm up today?"

"I'd be happy to. But I can't stay past four. I have a previous appointment."

"Oh," she looked down. "Will you be there at my final?"

Her voice was so uncertain, so completely different from the confident woman he loved. He nearly choked on his own saliva. *Loved? Surely not. Not yet.*

"Trevor? It's really okay if you can't. No pressure, honestly."

Her rapid words made him realize the feeling of shock and panic must have reflected on his face.

"No, hey, sorry, it wasn't that. Yes, I plan on coming. Is there anything you want me to ask of you? You know a little reciprocation?"

She laughed nervously but shook her head.

"I'm not sure how it will turn out but just knowing you're there, will help. I only wish my family could make it."

He wanted so badly to tell her, but he kept it secret. She took his hand and smiled. "Thank you for being there last night and today. I'm so lucky to have a friend like you."

Friend. Right. That all he was to her.

"The pleasure is mine," he answered tightly and they both fell silent for the two remaining minutes until they reached the hotel.

Meeting Trevor's family was less scary than she thought it would be. There were dozens of O'Quinns, and she had no hope of remembering any of their names except his mother's and father's. She would know Trevor's dad, Emmet anywhere. His auburn hair was still vibrant, though some grey had snuck in its depths and at his temples. But he had the same laughing blue eyes and overall physique that Trevor had. The way he would take his wife's hand randomly and wink at her made Cassie's heart ache. Robbie had never done that, he hated public displays of affection. The way Trevor's stepmother so easily teased her husband and the soft kisses she gave him when she thought no one was looking, made Cassie wonder; would she ever feel comfortable enough with her husband to do that? What was their secret?

Looking over at Trevor, she envied his easy smile as he spoke with one of his aunts and the genuine look of interest in his eyes when one of his younger cousins asked him something.

Brunch went by too fast and soon Trevor said those long-awaited words; "We should be getting back. Cassie's jury is tonight at six and I promised to help her warmup."

"Absolutely," Mara, Trevor's stepmom said. "You will do so well, my dear. We were so impressed with your performance last night. And we look forward to your Christine Daaé."

"Thank you," Cassie smiled. "And thank you for brunch."

"Of course," Emmet said. "We're glad to have met you properly." He winked.

"Me too... meeting you, I mean."

"Is your family coming to your final?" Mara asked.

Cassie kept Mara's gaze but felt tears pricking the back of her eyes. Mara's brows furrowed and her eyes went to Trevor who saddled up to Cassie and wrapped an arm around her shoulders. His heat immediately comforted her.

"They couldn't make it, mum," Trevor told Mara. "Her dad is a farmer up in Longford. It's the end of lambing season."

"Oh, I'm so sorry, my dear," Mara took her hand. Cassie

smiled sadly at the older woman, but her mind was still on what Trevor had said. She had mentioned her family's farm in County Longford once, many years ago and one time her brother Padraig had come to Dublin to meet her and Trevor had agreed to take him out for a pint while she was in class, but she had said nothing about it being lambing season.

"That's too bad," Emmet said.

"Well, if you'll have us," Mara went on. "We would absolutely love to be there for you and cheer you on. I know we're not blood but you mean something to Trevor, so we love you. Beside with the forty-five of us, you won't be lacking fans."

Cassie looked around at all the people near them. Every single one was a member of Trevor's family. Growing up, she always thought her family was huge and close knit but seeing the myriad of faces and knowing all of them were there to support Trevor, did something to her heart. She wished to be part of something like that, overwhelming as it might be.

"I would love to have you all there," she said. "Thank you."

"Oh, no worries, my dear," Mara said taking Emmet's hand and giving him a look. She smiled and turned back to Trevor. "You two be careful. Remember, we sopranos warm up a little differently than tenors, but the basics are the same."

"How long have I known you, mum?" Trevor teased. "I know just how high maintenance you sopranos are."

"Ohhoho," Emmet took a step back. "I'm gettin' out of firin' range."

Mara was not a large woman, but she was hardly tiny. Though next to her husband, her five-foot six-inch frame was dwarfed by his, she placed her hands on her hips and pinned her stepson with a stare. Trevor's stupid grin grew wider.

"Ah, mum, you know I love you," he said.

111

Mara's pursed lips fought a smile at Trevor's wiggling eyebrows. Finally, she couldn't resist any longer and broke into a grin.

"Just like your father," she shook her head. Trevor and Emmet shared a look and with a cheer, Trevor engulfed Mara in a hug, lifting her up.

"Tiss, put me down," she teased, smacking his shoulder.

Emmet merely watched from a safe distance. As Trevor and Mara teased each other after he set her down, Killian and Aiofe walked over and joined in. Emmet headed to Cassie.

"That's my heart right there," he said, his eyes on his wife and children.

"Trevor said you and Mrs. O'Quinn have been married about twenty years?"

"Nineteen years, seven months," he answered. "The best days of my life."

Cassie bit her lip, seeing the sheer love behind his eyes as he stared at his wife. Emmet shook himself out of his thoughts and looked at her.

"How about you?" he asked. "Anyone in your life?"

"My boyfriend and I just broke up, last night," she admitted.

"I'm sorry to hear that," Emmet answered, his tone comforting.

"It's all right," she shrugged. "I need to focus on me."

"That's important," he agreed. "Never let a relationship get to the point you don't take care of yourself first. If you don't, you won't be able to take care of the other person."

Cassie let his words settle in her mind and said nothing. Trevor turned to look at her and she nearly stopped breathing. His smile was radiant and his eyes so full of... love. He winked and her knees nearly buckled.

"Trying to steal her, dad?" he called.

"I've already got an amazing woman," Emmet replied. "But this one is up for grabs." With a wink to her, Emmet pulled his wife back to him and kissed her.

"We should get back," Trevor said.

"Of course," Emmet agreed. "We will see you tonight, Cassie. We wish you well. And as they say in show biz, *break a leg.*"

With a sweet smile, Emmet draped his arm around his wife's shoulders, and everyone said goodbye to Trevor and Cassie.

Chapter
Sixteen

That evening, Cassie waited in the wings of the recital hall stage. After brunch with Trevor and his family, they utilized the empty recital hall to warm up until Trevor got a text around a quarter to four. He had the same stupid grin on his face from when they were in the bus. He told her she sounded great and then, after he hugged her, promised he would be at her recital, and left.

Now, she waited until the audience took their seats and with a deep breath, she confidently walked out onto the stage to the roaring cheers of the audience. Smiling, she knew Trevor's family were the loudest ones. With a nod in thanks, she looked up at the judges sitting at their usual spot, their muted lamps clamped to the table, her score sheet before them.

She thanked everyone for coming, even though she

couldn't see past the first row of the audience with the stage lights beating down on her. With a nod to her accompanist, she began.

Throughout her final, she was too focused on signing and getting through the judges' tests to look for Trevor. Wishing she could see more of the audience, she decided she would sing her heart out... for him. He always believed in her. When she completed the judges' test and was finally finished, she took one more bow, relief, and happiness racing through her. Coming up out of her bow, the house lights lifted, and she locked eyes with her mom, three rows back, applauding as tears streamed down her face.

"Mum?" she questioned. Her mom's smile grew. "Mum!" she cried and raced off the stage and into her mother's arms.

"Oh, sweetie," he mother's American accent soothed. "You were so amazing."

"I'm sorry, I'm so sorry I didn't tell you."

"Shh, shh, it's okay, sweetheart," she said. "We're here."

"How?" she pulled back and hugged her brother Padraig.

"We drove," Padraig winked and hugged her tightly. "It's so good to see you, sis. You sang beautifully!"

"I couldn't agree more..." Robbie's voice pulled her from her family. Turning, she saw him standing in the aisle.

"Robbie? What are you doing here?"

"Can't I support my girl?" he asked. She was speechless. He huffed. "I'm so sorry, Cassie," he said, not saying any more about their breakup in front of a crowd. "I'm so sorry I never supported you before, but I promise I will always support you from now on. You are amazing, baby." He reached for her and like a weird pull, she stepped closer. He lowered his voice to a whisper. "I have treated you like a bastard, I can't apologize enough for it, but I can change. I have changed. I can only hope you find it in your heart to give me another chance. I love you, Cassie and I want to make this work."

Cassie was stunned. He had never said those words to her but before she could say anything, he kissed her and turned to her mother.

"You must be Mrs. Doyle," he said, tucking Cassie under his arm. Cassie's mom and brother looked at Robbie, then Cassie then back again. "Robbie McConaghy. I'm your daughter's boyfriend."

"Oh," her mom said, looking at Cassie again then giving Padraig a side glance. "I'm sorry, Cassie never mentioned you."

"I'm so sorry," Robbie continued. "We've been wanting to try and come up there to see you all but with school and the finals it's been exceedingly difficult, so it has. I know she misses you. And... you must be her brother." He turned to Padraig.

"Yeah. Padraig."

"Good to meet ya, mate," he offered his hand to Padraig and pulled him into a backslapping hug.

Cassie could not believe the change in Robbie. It was like he was an entirely different person. Feeling her mother's eyes on her, she met her gaze for a moment, forced a smile and looked past her to see Trevor. He was staring at her, stone faced. When he met her gaze, he looked away, gathered his raincoat, and pushed his way out the door. His family already left.

Cassie said nothing to Robbie as he and Padraig talked about hurling, Ireland's famous sport. Her mom nodded once, and Cassie rushed out of the auditorium and through the main door.

"Trev—" she started but cut off when she saw he was surrounded by his family, his back to her. Everyone looked over at her, but Trevor said and did nothing. Mara looked at her stepson, then her husband, and finally stepped forward.

"You sang beautifully tonight, my dear," she said. "I am sure the judges will have nothing but good things to say."

"Thank you, Mrs. O'Quinn," she replied but hardly looked at her. "Trevor?" she asked.

He finally took a deep breath, his back rising and falling with the effort. He turned to look at her and she gasped when she saw the look on his face. He looked... broken.

"Trevor?" she asked again. Then just like that, his face returned to neutral, empty. "Thank you," she stated.

His brows furrowed. "For what?" his voice was rough, raspy.

"I know it was you who called Padraig. I know it's because of you my family was here today."

Trevor said nothing for a long moment then, "you sang like an angel tonight."

"Thank you for being there."

The side of his mouth lifted in a sad smile. "What are *friends* for?" he asked. Then with a nod, Trevor turned and walked through his gathered family.

"Trevor?" she called once more. He said nothing and continued down the sidewalk.

"Trevor," his father called, but again he didn't stop. Emmet turned back to Cassie and after a moment, he spoke softly. "You sang beautifully tonight, Cassie. Congratulations. I look forward to hearing you again as Christine Daaé."

"Thank you," she said. "Mr. O'Quinn, please, I need to talk to him. Please have him call me."

Emmet said nothing, only pursed his lips together and turned.

A blonde man, about Robbie's height who Cassie had met early that day but couldn't remember his name, walked over to Emmet, and spoke in low tones, his American accent showing.

"Uncle Emmet, we can't just—"

"Let's go, Peter," Emmet stated. "It's not our fight."

Cassie's brows furrowed. *What did that mean?* But before she could ask, they were all walking away. She was alone in the courtyard, the rain whipping around her as she watched the O'Quinn clan leave through the main archway of the university and out to the main road.

"Cassie?" Robbie's voice behind her made her turn around. He was holding the door for her, a sweet smile lifting his lips. "They're calling you back, love."

"What are you doing here, Robbie?"

He looked down and a look she had never seen before entered his eyes, shame.

"I know I've not been the best, nor even a good boyfriend to you, Cassie. But one thing I realized when I sat at my parent's table, my brother on one side, his fiancée not welcome at our family dinners, my parents miles apart from each other, is I didn't want to live like that. I want you by my side. I love you..." she stared at him. "You don't have to say it back, I know I don't deserve it. But I hope one day you will. I will do everything in my power to deserve your love, starting with supporting you."

"I need time," she answered.

"And I freely give it. But the judges want you back."

"Fine," with one final look back to where Trevor left, she headed back inside the recital hall.

Chapter Seventeen

Of course, of-bloody-course. Why does that not surprise me? I do one good deed for someone I love, and this is what happens. No good deed goes unpunished. But damn it all to hell!

Opening the door of his flat, Trevor looked around the room. His eyes fell on the bed, still unmade from when he and Cassie woke that morning. Her perfume hung in the air. The plate she ate her eggs off of the night before, lay on the drying rack.

Suddenly, Robbie's smiling face flashed in his mind and the way he was playing Cassie, the fake attitude. Trevor couldn't stomach it. Cassie was blind to him. She was blind to Trevor and blind to Robbie's ways.

Anger flowed fresh and hot through him with the speed of

a lightning flash. With a shout, he swooped his arms across the desk by the window and everything crashed to the floor.

Stalking to the bed, he ripped the sheets off the mattress and threw them toward the door. On his way across to the bathroom, he grabbed the mug of coffee and the plate she used and threw them against the far wall. They shattered and the remaining coffee streaked down the exposed brick, puddling on the floor.

Advancing to the bathroom, Trevor found the towel she used, hanging over the rod and, ripping it off, he headed to the door where the sheets were flung. Gathering them all up, he marched down the hall and shoved them all into the trash shoot.

Back at the flat's door, he barged in and stopped dead in his tracks when he saw his father sitting on the couch waiting for him.

"No," was all Trevor said.

"You don't know what I was going to say," Emmet answered calmly.

"I don't need to," he replied and started for the kitchen to get a broom to sweep up the broken bits of manufactured pottery.

Emmet stood and cut him off. Trevor tried to go around him, but his father and he may be the same height and similarly built, but Emmet would always be a bigger man in Trevor's eyes, and he stopped.

"I know a little about heartbreak, son," Emmet stated ironically when Trevor stopped moving and stared at a point over his father's left shoulder. "You are not alone."

The ball of agony that had gripped his heart and sat like a lead balloon in the center of his chest constricted. Trevor let out a gasp of pain. That was all the wound needed. Soon, he could not control it. Tears rolled hot down his cheeks and the ball of heartache, jealously, betrayal, and hurt released in a flood.

Trevor sank to his knees, his legs unable to support his weight. Emmet caught him and knelt with him, holding him close, absorbing the grief and giving him strength. Emmet said nothing, not that Trevor would have been able to hear it, his sobs wracked his body and echoed throughout the studio apartment. Guilt and shame coiled in his belly as he imagined what his father thought of his outburst. It wasn't very... manly.

"None of that now," Emmet soothed as if he heard his son's thoughts.

When the worst of the pain eased, Trevor pulled back and looked up into his father's blue eyes rimmed with compassion and sorrow. Emmet pushed back some hair from Trevor's face. "I would never think any less of you, you know that, right? Besides, I've cried like this myself when your stepmum left me all those years ago. I loved her so much," Emmet locked eyes with him.

"I love her, dad," he admitted. "God help me, I love Cassie and she'll never want me the way I want her."

"You don't know that, Trev."

"Yeah, I do. I've lost her forever."

Emmet tightened his hold on him. They said nothing for a short time, but soon, Emmet's voice filled the room again. "Come back to St. Helen's with me. Don't stay here. It wouldn't be healthy. Not after you..." he looked toward the sheetless bed.

"We didn't, I mean we slept together but that's all we did. Sleep."

"You are a grown man, Trevor. You don't have to tell me anything. But come with me. We'll get you your own room or you can bunk with one of your cousins. Peter has a double room. We weren't sure if Geoff was coming with him."

Trevor weighed his options. Anything would be better than sleeping, or not sleeping, in his flat with the memories of Cassie. He eventually nodded.

"Okay. You're right. I can't stay here."

Helping him to his feet, Emmet wrapped his arms around him. "I love you, son."

"I love you too, dad.

"Everything will be all right."

Trevor nodded, even though he knew his father couldn't possibly know that for certain. Walking to the chest in the corner, near his bed, he grabbed out his old traveling backpack and stuffed a few pairs of underwear, socks, his swim trunks, a pair of jeans, and a couple t-shirts inside. Might as well make the most of it if he was going to stay at the hotel. Turning off the lights and making sure the central heating was off, he turned toward his father standing by the door. One last look at the empty bed, he shut the door, locking it before walking down the hallway with his father, hailing a cab, and heading toward the hotel.

Cassie sat in Robbie's bathroom, taking a moment to herself after having just gotten rave reviews from the judges. One weight lifted from her shoulders just for another to be placed. Robbie's declaration of love was unexpected but seemed genuine. However, Trevor's look of emptiness and... betrayal haunted her. He had done so much for her.

Still, he only considered her a friend as was made clear by his declaration; *what are* friends *for?* And the fact he didn't kiss her when she wanted him to in his flat the previous evening.

Before she could sort her emotions or understand the motives of the two men surrounding her, a soft knock sounded on the door.

"Who is it?" she asked.

"It's me, sweetie," she heard her mother say.

"Oh," she smiled and unlocked the door. "Hiya, mum."

"Oh, sweetie," she replied when she entered the small room and closed the door. Immediately, she was in her mother's arms. There was no better place to be than in a mother's embrace.

"I missed you so much, mummy," Cassie said.

"I missed you too, my baby," her mother cooed. "Your dad was so sorry he couldn't make it but there's a few more lambs ready to give birth, he had to stay."

"I'm so glad you and Padraig could come."

"You have Trevor to thank for that."

"I know," Cassie looked down.

"Honey, tell me... who is Robbie? I didn't know you were dating anyone."

"I know," she said again and sat on the covered toilet seat in a huff. "Robbie and I have known each other for a little while, but we've been dating since Christmas."

Her mother nodded and leaned against the sink.

"Initially, it was amazing but, things changed," she couldn't bring herself to say why. If Robbie actually changed, she didn't want her mother to think badly about him. "But things seem to be better now."

"Honey," her mother said cautiously. "What about Trevor?"

"He's a great friend," she answered.

"You do know he doesn't think of you as merely a friend, right?" her mother asked.

Cassie looked up at her, searching her face. Eventually, she shook her head.

"It doesn't matter," she said. "I think that is irrevocably damaged."

"Nothing is irrevocable, love," she answered. "Not unless someone has passed away. Until then they have two ears to hear, one heart to feel, and lips to tell the truth. Do you care for Trevor?"

"I do," she admitted.

"Do you care for Robbie?"

"He told me he loved me," she explained. "Am I to throw that away simply for someone who has never admitted his feeling for me?"

"It's scary, I know believe me," she replied. "Coming to live in a new country where I knew no one but my husband. I know scary. But what you have to ask yourself is, is the scary *unknown* better than the unexceptional *known*? Once you answer that, my love, then and only then will you be able to choose what is best for you and no one can make that decision for you."

Cassie sat thinking about her mother's words for a moment longer, then forced a smile and stood.

"I don't know what to do," she sighed.

"And that's all right. There's no rule written that says you have to decide today," she said. "But let's go celebrate. Your brother and I are staying another few days. I know you have classes Monday and Tuesday, but maybe we can meet up after that?"

"Actually, I only have one more class and it's Wednesday.

The classes for the rest of the week are already done. I only have one more final this week, then graduation."

"Oh wonderful!" she smiled broadly. "We are so proud of you. Your father wants to be here for your graduation but just in case he can't be, know Padraig and I will be here and maybe we can bring one of your sisters too."

"I would love for you to all be here, but I know da's worry about the lambs. It's okay if he can't."

"I know that and so does he. You've never been selfish, love. But he wants to be here so badly."

"I miss him," she replied.

"He misses you too," her mom said. "But enough, hey, hey, no crying. Listen, maybe you and I can go shopping a little? It's been forever since I've been to the city. I know Padraig and Trevor are supposed to go to the pub sometime this week. Maybe we can go shopping while they visit?"

Cassie bit her lip refusing to ask when her brother might meet up with Trevor. "I know Robbie has offered to take us out to dinner tonight to celebrate. I'll ask him when he wants to leave."

"He said reservations are at eight, we'll need to leave soon. Honey," her mom looked down. "Do you know how fancy it will be? I didn't have much time to pack and I don't have much, as you know."

"Knowing Robbie, it'll be someplace extravagant," Cassie said. At her mom's wide-eyed gaze, she placed a loving hand on her arm. "You can borrow one of my black dresses. It'll be fine, mum."

"I don't want you ashamed of me."

A pang of guilt hit her heart. She straightened to look her mom head-on and waited until she raised her eyes to hers. "I could *never* be ashamed of you."

Her mom smiled slightly but nodded and with a final look at her daughter, they left the bathroom to see Robbie in the living room wearing dress pants and a shirt Cassie was sure cost more than her monthly earnings as a guide in the Long Room and Old Library.

Her brother stood with him, a cut tumbler of Irish whiskey in his hand. His eyes met her, and he forced a smile. Unsure what that look meant, Cassie headed over to Robbie and he greeted her with a small kiss.

No matter how much she tried, she still felt empty and her mind kept drifting to Trevor and what he was doing at that very moment.

Chapter Eighteen

Wednesday morning, Trevor woke slowly when he felt the body beside him move. His splitting headache was a token of the vodka shots he had lined up at the pub the night before.

Opening his eyes, he promptly shut them when the sun pierced through the blinds. He moved away only to hear a soft feminine moan beside him. Opening his eyes again, he looked beside him to the dark-haired woman sharing his bed, her head on his chest. Panic for a split second flooded him but soon flashes of the previous evening entered his mind.

The pretty brunette he approached at the pub looked too much like Cassie but he didn't care, the vodka shots they did together, the hot and heavy make out session in the back of the bar, the quick taxi ride to his flat, and the night of drunken passion they shared. But he couldn't for the life of him remember her name.

When he eased her head off his chest and got out of bed, he breathed a sigh of relief when he saw the open condom wrappers. He loved his father but one thing he had learned from him was to always, *always* use protection, so he didn't end up with a child of his own he knew nothing about. Staggering to the bathroom, he stopped off in the kitchen to grab a couple pain killers and a full glass of water. His eyes caught the brunette's when he exited the bathroom five minutes later. A soft smile on her face.

"Good morning," she said, her accent, French.

"Morning," Trevor replied, his voice rough from sleep and his hangover.

They both stared at each other for a moment, then the woman looked down.

"I don't mean to be rude," she started. "As much as I remember I enjoyed last night... I can't remember your name."

Trevor breathed a sigh of relief.

"I thought it was just me," he said.

She laughed and shook her head.

"Trevor," he reminded her.

"Martine," she replied.

"Of course," he nodded. "I think I made some quip about a martini."

"Did you? I honestly don't remember."

"I don't normally have such bad pickup lines," he replied.

"I've heard worse," she shrugged. She sat up fully and held

the new sheets he had purchased a day ago around her chest. "I should get going."

"Yeah, of course," Trevor said, he looked around the room, found her dress, and handed it to her.

"*Merci,*" she replied. "Thank you for being so pleasant about this."

"No worries, I'm sorry I don't have anything to offer you for food. But if you need some pain killers, I have that."

"I'm all right, maybe a glass of water," she asked.

"Of course," he turned to the kitchen and took his time, allowing her to pull on her dress.

"You can turn around now," Martine said. Trevor brought her water and waited until she finished it. "Thank you." He nodded and she kissed his cheek. "From what I remember, it was fun."

"Yeah," Trevor answered. "Was."

"If you're ever in Paris, look me up," with that, she left the flat and he sat on the bed.

It was Thursday. He had finished all his finals the day before and first rehearsal for *Phantom of the Opera* was Monday morning after their graduation in three days. Trevor had not seen Cassie since her jury. She had called him, but he declined the call and ignored her texts. Padraig had texted early that morning saying it was his last night in Dublin and was hoping to meet up with him. Trevor had promised a pint at the pub but wasn't sure if he could see him without talking about Cassie and Robbie. Still, he never wanted it to be said he reneged on his word. Grabbing his phone, he texted Padraig back and offered to meet up at seven. His stomach rebelled at the idea of drinking anything remotely resembling alcohol, but a promise was a promise.

After a shower and a change into clean clothes, his

headache eased but he was starving. Breakfast. Full Irish was the cure for a hangover. Heading to his favorite breakfast café just off the college campus, he was shown a chair at the bar almost instantly and ordered his usual.

One thing he missed was American bacon, but he was able to get the next best thing, back bacon. As he drank his orange juice, he glanced at his phone. His father had sent him a text the night before. His family had left Dublin Monday night and Emmet was reminding him not to do anything rash.

Well, a one-night stand definitely fell into the *rash category.* Typing out a text to his father so he didn't worry, Trevor sat back as his breakfast was set before him.

He had settled in to eat and read the news off his social media app when he heard a familiar laugh. The hair on the back of his neck stood on end and slowly, he turned toward the sound. At the door, waiting on a table, was Cassie, Robbie, Padraig, and Mrs. Doyle. The acid churning his stomach from the excess alcohol threated to eject when he sat their hands intertwined and her other hand on his arm, laughing and looking up at him like he was the best damn thing she could ever have asked for.

Putting his head down and focusing on his phone, he justified that he was not a coward, he simply didn't want the issue. They were seated and, already nearly halfway done with his breakfast, he motioned for the waiter to ask for his bill.

He should have known he wouldn't get away that easily. Padraig's voice called to him. "Trevor!"

Trevor closed his eyes but forced an amiable smile. Turning, he locked eyes with Cassie sitting next to Robbie, his hand in hers resting on her lap. The immediate anger surged but he was able to suppress it and looked over at Padraig who was waving him over. Giving the twenty-year old a small wave, he turned back to his food, no appetite any longer. After a moment, a hand came down on his shoulder. Looking over, Padraig stood beside him.

"Heya," he said. "Wanna join us?"

"Ah, cheers, mate," he said. "But I'm just finishing up. I'll see you tonight."

"I'm looking forward to it. Any chance to get away from Robbie and his sickeningly sweet attitude toward mum and Cassie. I swear I think he's hiding something. No one is that nice," Padraig stated.

Trevor said nothing. If Cassie hadn't told her family about Robbie's behavior, it wasn't his place.

"Yeah, sounds good."

"You all right?" Padraig asked.

"A little hungover," Trevor admitted.

"Ha, yeah I understand. Been there, like," he said. "We won't have many tonight."

"Just keep me away from the vodka," Trevor replied.

"Yikes, I will do. Well, I better get back. It was good to see you. I was hoping you'd swing by one of these days, but I'm glad we can meet up tonight. See you at seven."

Trevor nodded once and watched him walk back to his family. Mrs. Doyle gave him a smile, but Cassie and Robbie were too busy talking to look over. He paid his bill, took one more swig of his orange juice and left the restaurant. They were literally everywhere, and it was only going to get worse.

His final exams were over, he was free of school and would walk at graduation that next weekend but instead of being free to go home and hopefully never seeing Robbie McConaghy again, he was going to be forced to see him every day until the *Phantom* was over.

Trevor nearly punched the screen of his laptop yesterday when the cast list was sent out and there was Robbie's name in black and white below Cassie's, below his. That bastard was cast as Raoul, Christine's love and third major character.

Drowning his sorrows was going to do nothing but hurt him and his family. Instead, as he walked out of the restaurant and into the beautifully sunny day, he decided the best thing to do was to put all the pain and anger into his character. If he could channel the agony of losing something he loved into the angst of the *Phantom of the Opera,* he would give one hell of a performance and it would be a show everyone would remember. Perhaps, just perhaps it would help him get over the woman who was stolen from him.

Chapter Nineteen

Trevor opened the door to the pub across from his Grafton Street flat. Scanning the area, his eyes lightened on Padraig sitting at the bar, a pint in hand, watching the game on the television.

Trevor took a deep breath and for the briefest moment thought about leaving. Padraig hadn't seen him yet and he could rush across the street, back to his flat, send him a text, and apologize for skipping. But he didn't. Padraig didn't deserve it. He had been a friend and though Trevor was angry at Cassie and Robbie, he couldn't take it out on him.

Padraig looked over at the door, his eyes catching Trevor. He smiled, waved, and indicated the beer in his hand. Trevor forced a smile as the light caught his hair and eyes at just the right angle. Padraig looked the spitting image of his sister. Shaking the thoughts of leaving out of his head, he headed over to him.

"Heya," Padraig slid off the stool and gave Trevor a back-slapping embrace. "Good to see ya. I wasn't sure you were going to make it."

Trevor grimaced. "I wasn't sure meself, honestly."

Padraig nodded slowly. "It has more to do with my sister than the hangover you've been nursing all day, aye?"

Trevor sighed. *Here we go.*

"I get it," he spoke again before Trevor had a chance to say anything. "She seems a bit blind to you."

"I'm not the only one," he grumbled and took a seat on the stool next to the one Padraig had just abandoned. The bartender came over to take Trevor's order and a refill for Padraig as he slid back onto his stool.

"So, what's the story with Robbie and my sister?" he asked.

Trevor kept his sigh silent but was grateful to see the bartender filling his order. "I don't know what you mean."

"Oh, come on, Trev," he turned to him. "Anyone with eyes can see she's scared of something. Walking on eggshells around him. She stopped talking to us for nearly six months. We didn't even know she had a boyfriend. Honestly, ma and I thought you two were together after you called Sunday to let us know about her concert."

"We're just friends." Thankfully, his cider was placed before him and he turned to Padraig. "Sláinte."

"Sláinte," he clinked his glass to Trevor's. They toasted and drank. "But seriously. You need to tell me what's going on."

Trevor turned away. What was he supposed to say? *I'm in*

love with your sister and that bastard is abusive? It wasn't his place. Taking another gulp, he finally answered.

"All I can say is, you need to talk to your sister."

"She won't talk to me," Padraig grunted.

"Give her time. Robbie has a very... strong connection to her."

Padraig turned to him again. "Tell me one thing... has he hurt her?"

Trevor froze. Staring into Padraig's eyes, the boy was too perceptive.

"Trev?" he pushed.

Trevor took a deep breath and looked away. "Look, you need to talk to her."

"That bastard," Padraig breathed. "Why is she still with him? Why haven't you done something about this?"

"Look, your sister is a grown woman and can make her own choices. God knows she has. I am her friend, but I can do nothing."

Padraig huffed. "She chose him over you?" Trevor took another drink but said nothing. "I'm sorry, mate, I shouldn't have..."

"No, you shouldn't have," Trevor replied. "But I know why you did."

"I'm not angry at you. Just the situation. I don't understand how she could go back or stay with someone like that. Not when she could be with someone like you who actually cares for her."

"I've been asking myself that for months."

"I'm sorry, Trev. I know you care about her and I shouldn't

have accused you of not doing anything."

"No, you're right, but you love your sister. You're looking out for her. It's all right."

"I just feel so helpless all the way in Longford."

"I know," Trevor replied.

"Man, I know she's my big sister, but I'm the oldest boy and we're only two years apart. I want to make sure she's okay."

"I get it."

"I know you do. Keep an eye out for me? Watch out for her?"

Trevor took another drink. "I'll do my best, man. She doesn't make it easy. And if I'm honest, I'm not too happy with either of them."

"I know, but during the show? Please?"

With a sigh, Trevor nodded. "Of course, I will, mate."

"Thank you. Now, no more of that. How've you been?"

They talked well past Trevor's self-inflicted ten pm mark. After the heavy drinking, the night before, Trevor went slow and paced himself with water. Soon they were both growing tired and the evening was winding down. Half a beer left in their glasses, they stayed in comfortable silence for a short time.

The pub was getting crowded, buzzing with activity, when a group of young men, no older than early twenties walked in and crowded around the bar. Yelling for the bartender to fill their orders and all around causing a ruckus.

One of the men squeezed in between his friend and Padraig. Immediately, his nose wrinkled in disgust.

"Didn't realize we had such fragrance in our midst," the

man said.

Padraig immediately looked down.

"We got ourselves a pig farmer, lads," he continued taking his beer and turning to look at Padraig. "So, I've always wondered, do you live in a shithole or do you smell like that because you roll around with them?"

His companions laughed raucously. "Oink, oink," one of them said. Another snorted.

Padraig was giving valent effort to ignoring them, but Trevor saw the embarrassment on his heated cheeks.

"Hey," Trevor leaned over. "Enough, leave him alone."

"Ooh, is this your boyfriend? You like sausages, pig?" the first man taunted.

"I said enough," Trevor stated standing.

"Or what?" the first one questioned.

"Look, we don't want any trouble, just leave us alone," Padraig said.

"I don't think I will," the man answered taking a drink from his beer.

"I am so sick of guys like you," Trevor began.

"Trev, it's fine, just leave it," Padraig grabbed his arm and stood beside him.

"Listen to your boyfriend," the man winked. "Though I'm not sure how you could get over the smell."

Trevor stepped forward but Padraig's hand on his arm stopped him.

"Don't," he said standing. "He's not worth it." Padraig

looked over at the man and then back at Trevor. "Let's go."

The man puckered his lips and then grinned. Turning away from them, he turned back to his friend who slapped his back.

Padraig pulled Trevor out of the pub and into the street.

"The bastard, he had no right to speak to you like that," Trevor clenched his hand.

"I'm used to it," Padraig said.

"You shouldn't be and besides, you don't smell at all, the eejit."

"Trev, calm down, it's all right."

"Well, it shouldn't be," he shouted. "I should go back in there and teach him a lesson." He tried to walk back in. Padraig stopped him.

"Trev, stop," he grunted as Trevor tried to push past him as he held him back. "Look, I'm not my sister. He isn't Robbie. Your anger is misplaced."

Trevor stopped and looked at him. Again, he was struck by how similar he and Cassie looked. Taking a deep breath, Trevor nodded.

"It's okay," Padraig assured. "Trust me. I've been through worse. Being a sheep and pig farmer, the smells suck but it made me who I am. I am damn proud of my family and my profession. A lot of people would hate it if we stopped. They can't get enough of their sausages. And I have a feeling he's one of them, if you follow me." He winked.

Trevor breathed a laugh. "Yeah. But I still hate bullies. My stepmum's ex-boyfriend before she met da' was a bully. He nearly killed my da'."

"What?"

"Long story, but he wanted ma to suffer so he shot da' on the steps of the courthouse. It was touch and go there for a while. It just always made me hate bullies."

"Hey, I get it. But that guy was not worth our time. There are bullies that need to be ignored and those who need to be shut down. He falls into the former category. Let it go."

Trevor was still angry, and Padraig saw it.

"Thank you, Trevor for standing up for me but honestly... look, nothing I say or do will make you feel better. You know what my sister does when something bothers her? She sings her heart out on some aria about death or poisoning or whatever. Her favorite is the Queen of the Night's Aria. Can you get into the auditorium? I didn't get a chance to see your jury and I always liked hearing you and my sister sing together. Think you could sing an aria for me? And no, I'm not hitting on you," he chuckled. "I just think it would help you."

Trevor stared at him for a while, then sighed. In truth, he was itching to sing. He needed to do something and to avoid being arrested for causing a pub fight, singing was the best option. He could control that. He could maim, torture, or kill simply by choosing between Mozart, Wagner, or Puccini. Turning toward the university, Padraig followed instep beside him. He always felt better after he sang, like working a muscle that needed to be exercised. It released endorphins and he could use as much as he could get.

It would work. It had to.

Trevor walked up the steps of the concert hall stage as Padraig sat in the center of front row. Trevor looked through his phone to find a piece he could sing that would adequately convey his emotions. Finally, he found one. Turning, to the portable sound system they always kept on stage for the singing majors, he plugged his phone into the speaker and, taking a deep breath, he hit play.

When the opening of *E Lucevan le Stelle* from the opera *Tosca* began, Trevor almost wished he could go back in time and sing it for his jury. It was one of his favorites, but it sounded better with a full orchestra instead of a single piano, so he and his accompanist agreed not to use it. But now as the karaoke version filled the music hall, he opened his mouth and let the first few notes ring out.

In that moment, he knew beyond a shadow of a doubt it was the correct song for him to sing at that moment. He poured his heart and soul into it. Thinking of Cassie, her bruised face, the hand prints on her wrists and throat, the way she looked in his apartment, the way she snuggled against him as they slept in his bed, the way she felt in his arms as they danced at the masquerade, the look on her face after they sang *Oui c'est moi J't'aime* in the men's locker room, the soft feel of her lips on his as they kissed under the gilded eyes of the cherubs and Greek gods in the main hall, all of it came back to him as he sang.

As soon as he began the nineth stanza, and Italian words that translated to *forever, my dream of love has vanished,* a single tear rolled down his cheek. Frustrated with the emotional display, he wiped it away and continued with every strength and power left in his *spinto* tenor voice. Anchoring himself, he dug deep, breathed from his diaphragm, and felt the power behind the *fortissimo* notes. She had done that to him. He had always had a powerful voice but the pain and angst behind the final few notes surprised even him.

Finally, the aria was finished, and he merely stood there, frozen as he fought the emotions bubbling to the surface. Cassie would never be his and it was high time he realized that. He would never have the dream of his love. It had truly vanished.

"Wow." He heard Padraig breath from the audience. Opening his eyes, he felt the wet on his lashes and immediately wiped his eyes. Padraig stood clapping. "That was amazing." He called. "I mean, I knew you were good, but damn that was... wow."

"Cheers, mate," Trevor let out a breath and shook out of his emotions. Plastering a smile on his face, he trotted down the steps toward him. Padraig clasped his upper arm and smiled.

"Feel better?" he asked.

"A bit," Trevor laughed.

"Good," he grinned. "I'm always here to help," winking he smacked Trevor's arm. "It's late. I should be getting back to the hotel. Thank you for the beer and for standing up for me. I hope everything works out with you and Cassie. I could really see calling you my brother."

"Likewise," Trevor stated. "But hands off my sister." He winked.

"No fair. I don't even know her. Is she pretty?"

"She's sixteen. Hands off."

"Okay okay," Padraig grinned.

"Come on, let's get you back." Trevor slung his arm around his friend's shoulders, and they walked out into the night air toward the bus stop.

Chapter Twenty

Cassie waited for Robbie to close the door of his flat where she had been staying the last few nights. It was sad to say goodbye to her mum, dad, sisters, and brothers earlier that Sunday afternoon, but she was extremely excited to start rehearsal for *Phantom* Monday. Padraig was tense around Robbie during their visit and Cassie wondered what he and Trevor spoke about when they went for a beer the week before.

"It was good to finally meet all of your family," Robbie said as he headed to the refrigerator and pulled out a can of soda water. Offering her one, he popped the tab and drank.

Now that her parents and siblings had left, it was time for Cassie to uncover the truth behind Robbie's drastically changed behavior, especially toward her parents which he had called *lowly farmers* in the past.

"Robbie, you do remember that my family are farmers, right? And my mother is American. *A Yank. The Farmer's wife*," Cassie reminded him of the insults he had hurled at her before.

He looked away. "I do, Cas," he answered. "I remember every nasty thing I've said about them in the past. All I can say is, I'm sorry. I've had my prejudices but seeing my family... my brother's fiancée not even welcome at my parent's house for dinner, made me realize. I want to be nothing like them. Please, Cassie, forgive me and give me another chance. I know I have a long way to go to earn your trust, but I hope one day I will, and I want to waste no more time trying to earn it. You told me once, if you remember, trust is easy to come by, but a second chance rarely happens."

She remembered saying those words to her masked stranger at the Christmas ball. Her mind whirled with the new Robbie and how much he had changed, but still, she doubted his sincerity.

"Do you still have the mask?" she asked.

"What mask?" he asked.

"The Venetian mask you wore at the ball?"

"Oh, that one... sorry, love, it was a rental. I had to return it."

She nodded slowly, still questioning.

"We should get going if we're going to make it in time," he said, his eyes on the clock over her shoulder.

"Yeah, I'm just going to freshen up," she said. "Two minutes."

"No problem. Do you want me to pack any snacks? Tea?"

"Tea would be good, but they probably have some. No need to put you out."

"It's never a put out for you, sweetheart," he kissed her lightly as she walked past him to the bathroom. As she washed her hands, her eyes fell on the perfume he had given her. She used it sparingly, but it was already a third gone.

"Hey, babe?" she called.

"Yeah?"

"Where did you go to get me my perfume?" she walked out of the bathroom with the bottle.

"Hmm?" he looked up from the tea kettle. "Oh, that. Honestly, I don't remember the name of the town, it was so remote. But it was beautiful, all mountains, lakes, and flowers, like a postcard."

"Flowers?" she questioned. "You went during the winter, didn't you?"

He turned back to the kettle. "Yeah, well, I saw pictures while I was there. But it was still beautiful."

"When did you go? Right after the ball or a couple days later?"

"Why the questions?" he asked turning back to her. "Is it the wrong one?"

"No! Oh no, it's not wrong. I was just wondering. I wanted to go and buy more so thought we could go together, and you could show me where you went."

"Sure," he replied. "But wouldn't you rather go to the French Riviera? My parents have a villa right on the beach. We could even sunbathe in the nude, so we could," he wiggled his eyebrows. She laughed but shook her head.

"Not really, I'd like to go to Norway."

"Then love, for you, we go to Norway," he replied just as the kettle whistled. He pulled the boiling water off the cook top and poured it into a travelling mug with two tea bags. "Your tea, my lady."

"Thanks," she smiled tightly at him.

"Ready?"

"Ready," she replied.

Together they headed to campus for the initial read through of the musical. Cassie's nerves getting the better of her with thoughts of seeing Trevor again. She hardly had a chance to see him while at breakfast. Robbie had taken the aisle seat boxing her in so she could not go to him. She found herself jealous of her brother being able to talk to him and even touching his shoulder. She missed him. Her mother's words rang in her ears but how could she throw away the time with Robbie, a man she had fallen in love with that night at the Masquerade Ball even if she didn't know his face. The man he became was who she always thought he could be. No matter how much she *liked* Trevor, he was a friend and had never said otherwise. Still, she missed their times together, talking, singing, just being.

They arrived at the large classroom most rehearsals would be in until they moved to the theater and she kicked herself for immediately scanning for him. He wasn't there. The room was set up with eight-foot tables laid out in a large square. Their nametags faced the inside of the square where Professor Lipscomb's small three-foot by three-foot square table and chair stood.

Professor Lipscomb welcomed them both and offered the refreshments on the table to his right. They greeted a couple of their classmates and Robbie introduced her to some of his friends in the theater department. But every chance she got, her eyes drifted to the door waiting for Trevor to arrive. When he finally did, she wanted to be sick. The door opened and Trevor walked in, holding the hand of the woman who was playing Meg Giry, Christine Daaé's friend. He leaned down to hear what the first-year student was saying and laughed, then whispered in her ear. Cassie felt the whisper of his breath on her own ear and immediately, her cheeks turned pink with the memory of how his body had felt pressed against hers when they slept in his bed.

"Snack, love?" Robbie offered. She nearly jumped out of her skin and turned to him. "Okay? Sorry, darling."

"Fine. Sorry. Mind was elsewhere."

She saw Robbie's eyes flicker to where Trevor spoke with the professor. His eyes twitched but he forced a smile.

"No worries. They have some cheese and olives along with some sandwiches."

"No olives, remember, I hate them," she said.

"Oh," he replied, his face fell. "Sorry, I forgot that."

"It's okay." But it wasn't. Trevor remembered the flavor of Bulmers she drank, and they hadn't even dated. "It'll take some cheese and a sandwich, no mayo."

"I'll get you a bottle of water too. If you want to go ahead and find our seats, I'll find you," he winked.

"Thank you, Robbie," she said. He smiled and turned to the food. "No, Robbie," he looked back at her confused. She took a step toward him and kissed him. "*Thank* you."

His grin widened and he wrapped his arm around her, pulling her flush to him. "Anything for my woman," he said and kissed her once more. But it felt wrong. His chest wasn't wide enough, his shoulders weren't strong enough, and his nearly sweet scent of cologne wasn't musky enough. His stubble was too soft, almost like peach fuzz, and his lips were too thin. Shaking it off, she pulled away and stroked his cheek. With a final wink, he let her go and she walked over to one of the tables. Looking at the name tents, their scripts and scores were set out.

She and Robbie were seated together but Trevor was directly opposite her, across the empty space. He was already seated flipping through the script, his travel mug beside his nametag. As much as she stared at him, he wouldn't look up at her. He seemed fascinated by the script. She wasn't sure if it was because of the part, the writing, or simply because he didn't want to look at her. But enough was enough, she wanted to say hello and if he wasn't going to look at her, she would go over to him. Just as she turned to walk around the tables, Robbie was there with her plate and water bottles.

"I thought we could share a plate when I saw we were sitting together," he said. She stopped, stared at Robbie, and then forced a smile. Sitting, she opened the water bottle and guzzled a third of it, her eyes back on Trevor as the woman he entered the room with sat beside him and he brightened with a smile. Too late, she realized she was crushing the bottle as she stared at him and Robbie stared at her. Forcing yet another smile, she turned to Professor Lipscomb who stood in the center of the square and began.

Chapter Twenty One

Trevor felt Cassie's eyes on him all afternoon but could not bring himself to look at her. He had met the actor who was to play Meg Giry at the door. She was a first-year student and nervous for her first university read-through. She was cute and reminded him of his younger cousins and sister but then a wicked idea entered his mind and he offered to walk in with her.

"First read through?" he had asked. She looked up at him, her too large eyes growing even larger.

"Yeah," she answered breathily. "Not sure why I'm so nervous."

"That's normal," he replied. She was a cute kid, he thought with her blonde hair and deep blue eyes. She looked incredibly young and a lot like one of his cousins, his Aunt Keera's and Uncle Paddy's daughter. "I'm Trevor. Trevor O'Quinn."

Her cheeks tinged pink. "I know," she said. "I was at your recital jury. You are amazing," she gushed.

Trevor chuckled. "Well, thank you. What part are you playing?"

"Meg," she answered then shrugged. "I've been performing ballet since I was five."

"That's fantastic. You shouldn't be nervous. You'll own that role."

"Yeah, I'm not nervous about the show, it's just, I'm the only first year with a named semi main part. It's intimidating."

"Nah, you deserve it. Tell you what, let's go in together. That might help."

"You wouldn't mind?"

"Of course not."

"Thanks, I owe you," she eyed him up and down. No matter what her innocent face may say, she was no child.

"Not at all. You remind me of one of my cousins." There, that told her wasn't interested and from her crestfallen face, she got the message. Still, he offered his hand to her and they walked in hand in hand.

Walking in together usually wouldn't have been a big deal, but considering he was the lead and a graduated final year student, all eyes would be on him and it did help her get over her fear. It was fun and Trevor hadn't had *fun* in a while. When he saw the seating arrangement, he knew it would never work. There was no way he could sit beside Cassie all rehearsal. Heading over to Lipscomb, he made his case saying it would be easier to see Cassie instead of being beside her, a lie but it was better than the truth. Lipscomb agreed and had one of the assistants move him directly across from her.

He sat only feet apart from her, but it might as well be miles. For the sake of the show, he knew he would have to put his personal feelings aside and work with her... and Robbie... but he didn't need to do it yet.

Lipscomb called everyone to order and began introductions. "What we're going to do now," he said. "Is go around the room, introduce yourself, say what part you're playing, your year, your field of study, and something unique about yourself. We'll start with our stars."

Trevor groaned. He hated the *tell us something unique about you* clause that seemed to happen every first day of anything. Since he was the title start, he got to first.

"Ehm," he started. "Trevor O'Quinn, Phantom, I just graduated. My degree is music with an emphasis in voice and something unique about me... I'm half American and my stepmom is the lead female vocalist in *Celtic Spirit* so I pretty much was on the road whenever my dad and I could join her. She got me into the studio at a young age and I credit her with my love of music."

"Excellent, thank you Trevor. I must say, I am looking forward to hearing you sing again, especially as the Phantom." Lipscomb turned back to the rest of the cast. "He and Miss Doyle sang the title song for his jury final and I still have chills thinking back to how marvelous it was." Trevor thanked him and Lipscomb turned to Cassie.

"Cassandra Doyle, please call me Cassie. Christine Daaé, I also just graduated and have the same degree as Trevor, music with vocal emphasis. Something unique... I have wanted to play Christine Daaé since I was twelve."

"Really?" Robbie asked beside her. "How did I not know

that?"

"Because you don't know her, you arrogant bastard," Trevor mumbled quietly. Only the woman playing Meg sitting beside him heard and she looked over at him, questioningly. He waved it off and she turned back to Cassie.

"Absolutely fantastic, Cassie I am so glad we are able to give you the chance and I know I can speak for the entire faculty when I say we are very excited to have you as our Christine." The drama and music faulty seated at the tables nearest the front wall to Trevor's right, nodded in agreement.

Lipscomb turned to Robbie and Trevor's hand clenched instinctively.

"Robbie McConaghy, Raoul, and like both the others I also just graduated but I have a theater degree with voice on the side. Something interesting about me is I have been the lead in every play produced in the department for the last two years and though I cannot claim the principle role here today, I am looking forward to playing opposite my girlfriend for the first time," he grabbed Cassie's hand and held it, giving her a soft look.

It took everything inside Trevor to stop him from getting up and leaving the room. He had hoped the anger would subside but every time he tried to put it behind him, Cassie's bruised face and neck along with her tears, flashed through his head and he grew angry all over again. Angry she could go back to him. Angry Robbie could treat her like that and angry he never did anything about it before.

But soon the introductions were finished, and it was time to begin rehearsal. Trevor reveled in the excitement of a new show and soon he let go of the anger, even for a couple hours, but it was a reprieve from the incessant fury. He'd be damned if he let a man like Robbie McConaghy ruin his favorite musical and his chance to shine. God only knew what could happen because of the play. He had looked into grad schools even more the last couple days and the more he looked the more America sounded good. Talent scouts also usually attended the show so it was time to show what Trevor O'Quinn actually could do without Cassie Doyle or Robbie McConaghy in the way or holding him back. He would give the Phantom the performance of a lifetime.

Chapter Twenty Two

"Good, very good," Pierre Benoist called over the megaphone from the second row in the balcony. The ballet instructor from the Dublin company watched the dancers as they finished the large number at the beginning of the musical, the opera Hannibal scene. Since Trinity did not have a dance department, they hired the renown instructor to assist their dancers. Most of the women and a couple men were only ballerinas from outside academic experiences like the one playing Meg. Colleen was her name and as she stepped off the stage and saw Trevor standing in the wings, she smiled and waved. He gave her a thumbs up.

"For two weeks rehearsal, they look wonderful, Pierre, *merci,*" Professor Lipscomb said as soon as the instructor came back down to the main auditorium.

"Not bad at all. I'd take them for my company in a heartbeat," Pierre said sitting beside one of the other professors.

"Moving right along, Mr. O'Quinn, Miss Doyle, Mr. McConaghy?" The three of them stepped forward. Trevor had asked to wear the Phantom's iconic mask during his scenes to be sure he knew how his singing would be affected by the obstruction, but fortunately it wasn't uncomfortable and when he slipped the white plastic over the side of his face, he felt more like the Phantom than ever before.

"We are ready for *Wandering Child* followed immediately by *Bravo Bravo.* As you all know, this follows the graveyard scene where Christine sings to her father. Mr. O'Quinn, the stage will be set up with a built walkway directly behind you and you will be standing on that, above Miss Doyle and Mr. McConaghy. Miss Doyle, Christine is stage right, the grave will be projected on a black screen beneath the catwalk where Mr. O'Quinn stands. Mr. McConaghy, you will enter on Christine's line of *what endless longings.* I want you to start as if you were worried for her but relieved to see she is well, then you see the Phantom hypnotizing her. You enter from stage left. Orchestra, we are at two slash four dash five, second stanza, key change four measures before Phantom's first notes. We do have a lot of powerful voices here, so let's be strong, but Mr. McConaghy enunciate, for you are the only one with drastically different lyrics." Robbie nodded. "Excellent. We're going through this four times and then you are dismissed for your afternoon tea. Orchestra, ready?"

"Yes, Professor," the orchestra director and viola teacher stated from the pit.

"Grand, places, please. For now, Mr. O'Quinn, just stand upstage. That's right. Good. Maestro, when you are ready, take it away."

"Hey," Colleen walked over to Trevor, her duffle bag slung over her shoulder. He turned from gathering his raincoat and small backpack.

"Hey," he smiled. "I told you you would own this role. That was amazing."

"Thanks," she smiled. "Listen, a lot of us are going to Ruin for a pint and some dinner. Wanna join?"

"Oh, I would but I need to memorize Act Two before Wednesday," he said.

"So? You have all day tomorrow to do that. Come on, you've earned it. You were amazing today too. Just because you're playing a homicidal hermit doesn't mean you need to become one," she winked. "Hermit that is."

"Thanks for the clarification," he grinned.

"Besides, the guy I've been seeing for a couple weeks is coming and I wanted him to meet everyone."

"How can I say no now without sounding like a homicidal hermit?" Trevor questioned.

"You can't," she teased.

Throwing his hands up in the air, he sighed. "All right. I'm game. Couple pints, a sandwich, good company, let's go."

"Yay," she smiled and threw her arms around his neck. "I'm so glad you finally accepted one of my invites."

"Me too, and sorry if I gave off the impression of not wanting to join. It wasn't you or the cast. I just needed to keep a clear head and–"

"And you were avoiding two people who don't deserve you."

He opened and closed his mouth in surprise, trying to think of something to say.

"Oh, come on. I don't know the background but it's obvious. And if she doesn't see how much of a wonderful person you are, she's clearly stupid."

"Hey now, Cassie is a wonderful person. No need for that."

"And even now you defend her?" Colleen shook her head.

"I guess I do," he sighed.

"Does she know you're in love with her?"

"What do you mean?"

"It's obvious, Trev," she answered. "But I won't say anything. Come on, let's get a pint. Sorry if I overstepped."

"It's fine," he said. "Like I said when we first met, you remind me of one of my cousins. You'll probably always be forgiven." He draped an arm around her shoulders and pulled her close. "Now, to scare your potential boyfriend so he knows you have someone looking out for you."

Rolling her eyes, Colleen elbowed his side. "I have older brothers for that. I only need you to look pretty."

"That's not challenging," he grinned.

"Cheeky," she teased. "But do give me your *guy opinion.* I'm getting really interested in this guy."

"I'd be happy to."

He smiled against the slight pang of sadness. He missed his family. It had only been four weeks, but he felt more alone than ever.

As he opened the door to Ruin Pub, he bit back his groan of disbelief. Robbie and Cassie sat together with some of the other actors. Colleen saddled up beside him.

"I'm sorry," she whispered. "I didn't know they were invited."

"It's all right. They're part of the troupe." He saw Cassie choke down a swallow of the regular Bulmers cider clearly not enjoying it. "Would you do me a favor?" He asked as they walked to the bar and ordered.

"Anything," Colleen said.

"Would you go give Cassie this?" He took the pear flavored cider bottle from the bartender and handed it to Colleen. She looked up at him, an indescribable look on her face.

"Sure." Taking it, she walked over to Cassie who looked up at her surprised. Colleen handed her the bottle, leaned down and whispered something in her ear. Cassie's eyes shot up to him and he raised his beer toward her. She smiled slightly at him but as Colleen walked back to him, Trevor glanced at Robbie only to find his eyes on him, a blank look in the dark blue orbs.

Looking away, Trevor walked over to the group of ensemble actors along with a couple stagehands and the two actors playing *La Carlotta* and *Signore Piangi*.

After a couple pints, Trevor was ready to leave but he headed to the restroom first. Once he finished and went to wash his hands, the door swung open and Robbie walked in. Trevor met his gaze in the mirror. The look on his face made Trevor prepare for a possible fight. Finishing washing his hands, Trevor dried them and turned to Robbie who had not moved from the door.

"Is there something you needed?" he asked calmly. "Or do

you make it a habit to corner men in the restroom?"

"I'm going to need you to stop flirting with my girl. I know you two have history as friends, and I understand that but it's getting out of hand," Robbie said.

"So, you want to control who she claims as friend as well?" Trevor asked.

"No, she's her own woman. She can make her own decisions, but I need you to respect that we are in a relationship."

"Here's the thing, Robbie," Trevor began. "You think no one can see through this little game of yours. This façade. But I can. And I remember. I remember the bruises on her face and neck. I remember the way you manhandled her out of the pub by the wrist you had already sprained. And we both know the truth behind your biggest secret. So, this little game you're playing? Consider this my ante in. You want to play? Game on."

Robbie's face morphed into an evil, smarmy grin. "You sure you want to do that?"

"Do your worst but cut the shit and be real for once. You don't even know her. It's pretty obvious you don't want to learn. I don't know what your end game is, but I will stop you if it hurts her."

Robbie leaned in close. "Good luck."

With that, Robbie left the restroom. Trevor took a deep breath. He needed to remain levelheaded and getting head over heels would not work. He needed a plan and a clear head. Pulling out his phone, he sent a text to his dad. He needed his family. Sending a plea for a long talk, he left the restroom, gathered his things, said goodbye to the remaining cast members, glanced at Cassie, and pushed open the pub door. The rain had picked up and as he shrugged into his raincoat, his phone rang his dad's ringtone, ready to talk.

Chapter Twenty Three

A couple days later, still without much of a plan on how to deal with Robbie, Trevor found himself back on stage, the set coming together nicely, with Cassie and Robbie. Several other cast members were seated in the auditorium.

"What?" Trevor questioned interrupting Professor Lipscomb as he was explaining the blocking for the climactic scene *Down Once More.* Lipscomb looked back at him, though slightly annoyed. "I'm sorry, professor. Could you repeat that?"

"At which time, Miss Doyle will grab you by the lapels and kiss you. I need you to be surprised she chose you…" His voice trailed off as Trevor's ears rang. *No, there was no way.*

"I'm sorry again, Professor, but shouldn't we wait on the

stage kiss?" he asked.

"Why?" Cassie asked.

"Whatever for, Mr. O'Quinn?" Lipscomb asked.

"Well, I'm a method actor," Trevor stretched the truth. "And if I'm truly to give a convincing reaction to a first kiss then shouldn't the actual first kiss be on opening night? And I'm sure her boyfriend would prefer it if she didn't have too much experience to compare him to." Robbie's face flushed with anger and Cassie's with embarrassment. "And besides, I'd hate to be a better kisser than her boyfriend."

Lipscomb chuckled ignoring the murderous glint in Robbie's eyes. But it faded and he placed his arm around Cassie.

"I don't think that's right, O'Quinn," Robbie started. "You're embarrassing Cassie. I have to call you on it."

Trevor bit back the response. His father had cautioned him to guard his tongue and pick his battles.

"It's not Cassie who's embarrassed, I don't think," he answered.

"Still," Robbie began.

"Stop," she hissed. "It's fine." Trevor had to prevent himself from puffing out his chest. "He's right."

"Very interesting idea, Mr. O'Quinn and I like it. Yes, Christine and the Phantom will not kiss until opening night. Now, places," Lipscomb ordered.

As Cassie walked over to Trevor and Robbie took his place on the stairwell, Trevor saw a different look on Cassie's face. He hoped to see disappointment that they wouldn't kiss. He never dreamt he'd see anger and a little hurt in her beautiful eyes.

Robbie smirked at him and Trevor read the resounding

message in his gaze: *Round one to Robbie.* Trevor overestimated his pull.

"Cassie," he started low.

"Enough. I really don't want to hear it," Cassie said.

"I'm sorry."

"You should be. I'm with Robbie. Trevor, why? How dare you embarrass me like that."

"I didn't mean to, I just—"

"What Trevor?"

"I was wrong. I... I'm sorry. I wasn't thinking."

She stared at him for a long moment. "What happened between us?"

He went rigid. "Nothing."

"It's clearly not nothing. We used to talk. We used to be friends," she said softly.

"Yeah," he spat. "Friends. We did."

"I'd like you and Robbie to be friends too. He's changed, Trevor. Aren't you happy for me?" She searched his eyes.

Seeing a lost cause, it broke his heart, but he gave up. "Yeah, of course I'm happy for you." Stone built around his heart.

"Thank you, now no more making me feel embarrassed. Got it?"

"Absolutely, got it." *Crystal clear.*

It was over until she discovered it was all an act and who Robbie actually was... and who he wasn't.

Chapter

Twenty Four

As opening night arrive, Cassie woke to Robbie in the kitchen pouring two cups of tea. Part of her hoped that if the past month and a half had been an act with Robbie that it never changed. He had been the best and sweetest man she ever met. Even when her father, the farmer, had come down to see them at graduation, he greeted him and treated him almost like a son-in-law.

But when he turned to her, smiling, and offering the teacup, she found herself remembering Trevor's smile instead. She frowned but then, sitting up, she accepted the tea and they sat together.

"Okay?" He asked. She smiled and sipped the tea nearly gagging because of the overuse of honey, but she choked it back.

"Yeah, great," she lied. "Can I ask next time just a little less on the honey?"

"Oh," her face fell. "Sure," he took it from her and headed back to the kitchen.

"No, Robbie, it's fine. I'll drink it."

"No, babe, I want it to be perfect for you. Gotta make sure you are in the best voice for today and if there's too much honey it won't be good." He washed the cup out and dried it before turning back to the cooktop and pouring more tea. Bringing it back to her, he offered her the honey for her to measure it.

After taking the first sip, it was perfect. "Mm," she hummed. "Thanks. Perfect."

"Good." He sat on the side of the bed and drank his. "Are you excited?" he asked.

"Nervous," she admitted.

"Don't be, you will be wonderful," he kissed her forehead. "But I'm sorry. I need to leave you. I have a ritual I always do during the day of Opening Night. It prepares me."

"Of course," she nodded. "I'm supposed to meet Lipscomb to go over a couple lines of *Think of Me.* I'll see you tonight?"

He smiled. And she was happy to think of how handsome he was.

"I wouldn't miss it," he winked. "I have a surprise for you."

"You do?" she questioned. He nodded and leaned toward her, resting his forehead on hers. "Won't you tell me what it is?"

"You'll have to wait and see," he replied. "But I don't think you'll be disappointed."

"When will I get it?"

"Impatient much?" he chuckled. She looked away and shrugged. Robbie pulled her chin back gently. "I'm glad. But you'll have to wait until we get to the theater."

"That's not long," she agreed. "I can wait."

"Good," he nudged her nose with his and followed the action with a kiss.

"I love you," he said softly.

"I love you, too," she answered. He pulled back and stared at her. "What?" she asked.

"Nothing," he shook his head. "It's just the first time you've said it." He kissed her again but pulled back before neither of them could stop thinking. "I have to go," he groaned.

"Right now?" she pouted.

"I'm sorry. I wish I didn't."

"So do I."

Robbie chuckled and stood. "I will see you at the theater."

"Only eight hours," she agreed. "Thank you for putting my family up in the hotel."

"It's my pleasure," he answered. "But now I must go."

She nodded and watched him leave the flat, curious what he was doing but knowing all actors have their rituals before going on stage. She ignored it, got dressed, packed her stage bag with a little black dress for dinner after the show and texted her mom. Robbie had invited her entire family out afterwards to one of the most exclusive restaurants in Dublin to celebrate. Over the past month and a half, Robbie had encouraged her to call her family nearly every day and her mother was always so happy to hear from her.

When Robbie told her, he had purchased three hotel rooms for her mother, father, brothers, and sisters to stay the weekend and attend Opening Night, she fell in love with him. Since then, she had been riding a cloud. Still unsure if he was her masked stranger, she gave up the ridiculous pursuit and learned more about the man by her side than the fantasy who still showed up in her dreams... dreams she ought not be having while sleeping next to Robbie.

Arriving at the theater, she entered the stage door and immediately heard a well-known voice singing *Music of the Night*. Trevor. She smiled when he hit the belted high note and the hair on her arms rose. Trevor embodied the character and she loved watching him. Lipscomb's voice came next as he stopped the orchestra and spoke to the strings section. Tiptoeing over to the wings of the stage, she watched. Trevor stood in the middle of set, stagehands working behind him, touching up one of the flies. He was looking down at his phone, but she was mesmerized. He wore a tight pair of dark jeans, a button up white shirt, open at the collar and a dark grey specked cardigan. Too late she realized she was biting her lower lip and all the feelings from before came pouring back. Her skin was too tight, and a heavy flush caressed her entire body.

"I'll be right with you, Miss Doyle," Lipscomb's voice broke her out of her thoughts.

Trevor's gaze flew to hers. She gave a small smile. He took a deep breath but gave her a nod. For a second, his eyes filled with a sort of longing but nearly instantly, his stony gaze was back. Ever since that moment he had tried to... she wasn't sure, tease her, embarrass her, with the kiss comment, their relationship strained but he was still kind and occasionally she would catch him staring at her. She wondered again if he and Robbie had talked. She wanted her boyfriend and best friend to be friends, but knew it was a lost cause. But just because she was with Robbie shouldn't mean Trevor kept his distance.

"Are we finish, Professor?" Trevor finally asked Lipscomb.

"Actually, since I have both of you here, I wanted to go over *Past the Point of No Return.*"

"I'm afraid I haven't warmed up yet, Professor," Cassie called.

"Mr. O'Quinn, could you assist her? I'll be with both of you shortly." Lipscomb's tone did not give either of them a chance to refuse. Not that she could have. It had been too long since they had been alone together. But Trevor looked as if he had just swallowed a bug.

Hurt bloomed in her chest and soon she was walking away and toward a warmup room below the stage. Trevor's steps followed her. As soon as she heard the door shut behind him, she turned a pair of scathing eyes to him.

"What is your problem with me, Trevor?" she demanded. "You go from being the sweetest man I know to an arsehole. Did you and Robbie switch bodies or something?" his eyes flamed, and his nostrils flared. "All I can think of is you are upset with me and I can't for the life of me understand why. This past month and a half, we were supposed to be Phantom and Christine. My dream and I had my best friend playing opposite me, only he was no longer my best friend because the man standing before me is a complete stranger. So, what the hell happened?"

I was like a dam broke. He stepped toward her. "You want to know what happened? I'll tell you. The second that bastard bats his eyes at you or crooks his finger in your direction, you go running. His temper be damned. The fact he abused you horribly, ignored, and the one person who cares about you the most, rejected. So, forgive me if I seem a little put out. After this show is over, you won't be bothered by me again."

"What the hell are you talking about? Trevor, I care about you and I want us to be friends."

"Just friends. That's the problem!"

"What is?" Her stomach somersaulted.

"You want to be just friends, when all I can think about is holding you in my arms that night. Comforting you. Sleeping beside you. Being there for you. All I want to do every waking moment is kiss you again, make love to you. Be the one you smile at, that causes you to smile. The one you want to be with. But no, you chose the one man who hurt you, over me. And now, I have to find a way to move on because it is clear you won't be interested in anything I have to offer, even if it's love."

Cassie stood frozen by the piano in the warmup room. She stared at the stormy blue eyes of the man she never knew she wanted. Trevor turned away from her for a moment, then looked back. His face contorting in pain.

"It's physically painful for me to be around you, seeing you with him. And knowing you don't see what I see. You don't remember what I remember. You know he cornered me in the restroom at Ruin that day we went? He told me to stop flirting with his girl. He said you were his. It was a game to him. I played for a time, but every time I tried, he outsmarted me because he's so damn calculating and manipulative. You don't see it. You never will. Padraig even saw it and asked me if Robbie abuses you. It wasn't my place, so I said nothing, but dammit, Cassie..." he huffed and thrust his hands through his hair. "Forgive me if I'm not the perfect little best friend you wanted. I can't be. Not any longer. Now, can we please get on with this, that way I can get out of your hair."

He moved to the piano and as much as Cassie tried to tell her hand to reach out to him, it stayed limp by her side.

Robbie had been amazing, and she could not, would not, sacrifice the man he had become for something unknown, no matter how much she may want it. He wasn't calculating. He couldn't be. She wasn't a game. She meant more to him; she knew it. She couldn't throw away the life she built with him.

Trevor sat at the piano bench and played his fingers up a chord run. Then turned to look at her and sighed harshly.

Finally, "I'm sorry," he said. "I didn't mean to raise my voice. And I didn't mean to keep my distance. You don't deserve my ire. It's just seeing you with him, knowing he put that bruise on your cheek, the handprint around your throat, and the tears in your eyes, makes me angrier than I have a right to be. Forgive me and please ignore what I said. It was said in anger."

Again, she said nothing, but Trevor looked back at the keys and began a chord progression to help her warmup.

Lunch was provided for the orchestra, but Trevor needed some fresh air. Going over several of the Phantom's and Christine's songs together, he needed a break away from Cassie. After his declaration in the warmup room, they had gotten over any awkwardness by the time they stepped out on the stage for Lipscomb. But nothing could cool him when Cassie put her heart and soul into their songs. She would find ways to randomly touch him. His hand, his leg, his arm, even once cupping his jaw. All her little touches grew a fire inside him.

A lunch away from everyone was what he needed. When three o'clock rolled around, he had to return. It took at least two hours for the makeup department to create the monster beneath the mask. He also had a little something he needed to pick up from his flat. Deciding it was as good a time as any to give Cassie the perfume he had picked up in Norway, he headed home, found the gift, still wrapped in the colors of his mask. As he walked back to campus, he passed a flower vendor. Stopping, he looked at each bundle, roses, daisies, sunflowers, dahlias, but what caught his eye were the red roses tinted slightly with black. Lifting the bouquet, they were the same deep color of the wrapping paper around the bottle he carried in his backpack.

"Do you have gold ribbon?" he asked the vendor.

"Take your pick," he laid out three spools of gold ribbon. Trevor's eyes fell on the wire lined, crimped thick gold ribbon. Asking for that one, he handed him the bouquet and payment.

"Any special way you'd like the ribbon?"

"Wrapped around the stems up to the flowers then a large bow with long tails," Trevor explained.

The vendor did as he asked and Trevor accepted the flowers, thanked him, and continued to the campus theater. He didn't run into anyone on his way to the dressing rooms, no one was there apart from one stagehand. Taylor had been with the cast since the beginning. Going out with them when they got pints or dinner together. She was a second-year student with a focus on stage management and technical theatre. She greeted him as he headed down the stairs. Her eyes turned to the flowers and give.

"How beautiful," she breathed.

"You didn't see me," he said. "But could you put this in Cassie's dressing room?"

Her brows furrowed. "I'm sure she'd want to know who gave her such a beautiful bouquet."

"No," he stated firmly. "I was not here. You did not see me. Please, Taylor."

She stared at him for a long moment, then sighed and nodded. "You know, he doesn't deserve her. Why don't you fight for her?"

"She doesn't want to be fought for," he admitted. "Just

please don't say anything."

She nodded again, took the bouquet and gift, and went into Cassie's dressing room. His task successfully completed, he headed to his dressing room and sat as still as he could as the makeup was applied.

Chapter
Twenty-Five

Cassie had not seen Robbie all day and after her interaction with Trevor, she was glad. It made her think. No matter how much Robbie had changed over the last month and a half, Trevor was right about him. He had hurt her. It was almost like she was waking from a dream and ugly reality was setting in.

Heading down to her dressing room around four-thirty, curtain was up at six, she stopped in the doorway when she saw a bouquet of red black tipped roses and a small wrapped gift. Curious, she walked over to see a card. The folded cardstock had her name on it. Flipping it open, she swallowed down the bile that rose in her throat.

Thanks for the dance. I always knew you would be the best Christine.

Yours,

Phantom

The roses were beautiful and the red, black, and gold mirrored the mask Phantom had worn at the ball. Smiling, she remembered Robbie's promise for a surprise. The roses were lovely, but she looked down at the small wrapped parcel. The wrapping paper looked a little worn but as she unwrapped it, part of her wanted to take her time and another wanted to tear into it.

As soon as the item was revealed, she felt a sense of dread churn in her belly. The feeling so sudden she felt lightheaded. Sitting down at the mirror, she stared at the box holding the bottle of perfume. For some reason, she knew that bottle was from her masked stranger, which meant Robbie was not the man she thought he was. He had lied to her.

But who? Who left this for her? It was almost as if she had her own *Phantom of the Opera.* Then a face flashed in her mind.

Trevor? No, not possible. He wasn't at the ball; he went home a week before. He had told her...

"Knock, knock," Robbie's voice came from the doorway. She turned to look at him. His brows knitted together. "Are you all right?" He entered the room quickly.

"Did you give me this?" she indicated the perfume.

His eyes grew wide. "No," he said. "Do you have a secret admirer I don't know about?"

"I'm beginning to wonder," she replied staring at the roses.

"Hey, it's all right," he knelt before her. "It comes with the territory, like. Someone probably heard how amazing you sounded and wanted to show you a token of their appreciation. And well deserved too, my love."

"It's like I have my own personal phantom."

"Well, then you have your own Raoul too," he winked.

She moved away from him and stood.

"Did you ever go to Norway?" The words were out before she could stop them.

"What?" he asked still kneeling before her chair.

"After the ball," she clarified. "Did you ever go to Norway? Or did you pay someone?"

Robbie looked down. "I couldn't get away, so I paid my father's secretary to go. But that does not change anything."

"It does," she scoffed. Robbie stood and rushed to her. Taking her hands in his, he waited until she looked at him.

"I love you," he said. "My methods may have been a shortcut, but I love you. I am still the same man you danced with at the ball."

"Are you?"

"What does that mean?"

"You lied about the perfume. Couldn't you have lied about dancing?"

"How else would I have known about it? Cassie, please, I love you. I should have told you about the perfume, but I didn't want it to change how we saw each other."

She looked up at him, her head spinning but seeing his blue eyes, she nodded slowly. She was letting the preshow nerves get the better of her.

"I'm, sorry, it was just a bit..."

"Freaky? I get it," he said and wrapped his arms around her. "I love you and I can't wait to give you *my* surprise."

"I'm not sure I can handle any more surprises," she mumbled into his chest.

"You'll like this one, I assure you."

She let out a laugh and looked up at him. He kissed her gently. A knock came from the door, then it opened.

"Oh, sorry," the makeup student set to do Cassie's makeup stepped back.

"No, not to worry, come on in," Cassie called then looked up at Robbie. "I love you. I'll see you at circle up."

Robbie bopped her nose and winked, heading out of the room.

Circle up was always fun. All the actors gathered in the green room in a circle, holding hands, their right hands holding the other's left hand, arms crossed their bodies. It was a time for actors to thank one another and calm any nerves they had before the show began. Usually led by the director, it was the last chance for any final thoughts or announcements. Trevor was actually happy to have a chance to stand next to Cassie. After their conversation earlier that day, he felt they had cleared the air. And though he stood in full Phantom makeup and white half mask, it still hadn't completely dawned on him that he was about to portray the *Phantom of the Opera*.

"I want to thank everyone," Lipscomb started from Trevor's other side. "This was a labor-intensive production but the way you all dived in made it so much easier for us all. Our leads, I want to thank you personally for being so flexible and working hard with each other," the three of them smiled. "It is hard to believe that six months ago the production professors and I stood in this very theater watching as the Masquerade Ball... in the terms of our lead... *took flight.* Seeing most of you there by the grand staircase and the white and gold gilded walls... I felt like I was at the Paris opera house here in Dublin and knew then I had to do this production. It was a magical night and I am so glad this story has come full circle. I know your fans will be waiting for you all and now doors are open, the house is filling up... no pressure but it is a full house tonight." He laughed at some of their groans. Trevor smiled. He couldn't wait. "Now, if there's no other announcements."

"Actually, Professor I have something I'd like to say," Robbie said from the other side of Cassie.

"Oh, of course, Mr. McConaghy, what is it?"

"I know there is an engagement ring for the show, but I was hoping maybe we could change it?"

"Change what?" Lipscomb asked.

"Well, I thought maybe we could use this one instead," he broke the circle to pull out a small box.

A hot chill ran down Trevor's spine and his heartrate skyrocketed. Watching in horror, he saw Robbie move in front of Cassie and get down on one knee. When Robbie opened the box, Trevor's vision went speckled when he saw the huge diamond ring, at least seven carats and surrounded by five other diamonds. His ears rang. He couldn't hear what Robbie was saying to Cassie at first but then he heard those words...

"Cassandra Doyle, will you marry me?"

Trevor listened to Cassie's response. She hesitated for a moment and part of him wondered what she would say, but then the word was out of her mouth and there was no going back.

"Yes."

When she saw Robbie kneel in front of her, all thought fled and soon she was staring at the most beautiful, though a bit big for her tastes, engagement ring. The gasps around her resounded in her ears but the silence from beside her, was deafening. Trevor did nothing. Robbie was speaking but she didn't hear, her ears tuned for anything from Trevor beside her. When Robbie finally asked the question, she took a deep breath. Now was the time to decide her future. She could refuse him and sacrifice the comfortable for the unknown and the show along with it, or she could say yes and live the rest of her days with the man before her.

Swallowing hard, she looked down at Robbie and just like the song they were about to sing, she was *Past the Point of No Return.* There was only one answer she could give.

"Yes," she answered. His smile was blindingly bright and as he stood and swept her up into an embrace and a kiss, the others in the room, apart from one, applauded.

"As wonderful as that is," Lipscomb clapped his hands once a couple minutes later. "We are at places everyone. Congratulations, you two. We will have more to celebrate with the champagne I've ordered tonight. Now… break a leg, everyone!"

They turned out of the circle and her makeup artist rushed to her, powdering her nose, and wiping her eyes. Everyone hurried around the room. Robbie, first on the stage as an older Raoul, headed to the stage with a kiss and a wink.

She looked for Trevor but did not see him. Hearing the initial welcome over the loudspeakers, reminding everyone to silence their phones and that flash photography was not permitted, she hurried to her dressing room for the final touches and her eyes fell on the perfume. Taking a precious two seconds to pull the bottle out of the packaging, she sprayed two squirts on her neck and another on her wrist. Then the music started. She ran up the stairs at the sound of the organ playing the overture. With a smile on her face, she headed on to the stage with the others.

Chapter Twenty Six

To hell with it all. She made her bed, let her lie in it. Trevor thought as he adjusted the mask on his face. The power of the overture music rattled the blood in his veins and with a deep breath in, he took in all the pain and anger and let it out in one long breath. Taylor, the stagehand who had helped him earlier, came up beside him as they watched the first scene of the opera within the musical.

"I'm sorry," she whispered. Trevor looked down at her. Her eyes never left the stage, but he knew what she meant.

"It was her choice."

She nodded and turned, placing a hand on his forearm. "Knock 'em dead, Trevor. You deserve this part. Do it proudly."

Trevor said nothing more, unsure if his microphone was on or not. But one thing was certain, he was not going to have to act much to portray the Phantom's heartbreak.

Trevor's performance was incomparable. Cassie had to tell him how amazing he was but if they weren't on stage together, one or the other of them was. Finally, it was intermission after one of the most emotional renditions of *All I Ask of You Reprise's* she had ever heard from an actor playing the Phantom. She knocked on his dressing room door. When she heard him call for her to come in, she opened the door quickly and closed it.

Trevor sat at his mirror, looking down at his phone, his head resting on two fingers, so he did not smudge the Phantom's makeup. He looked up and caught her eyes in the reflection of the mirror. Slowly, he leaned back and then turned in his chair to look at her.

In the second their eyes met, words failed her. She had never seen anyone look so... empty.

"I'm sorry," she finally choked out. "I just wanted to tell you how amazing you are."

He nodded slowly. "You too."

"Look," she started. "I wanted to also make sure we were okay."

"Okay?" he asked.

"Yeah, because of Robbie's proposal."

"It was your choice," he said. "I'm happy for you." Those words caused bile to rise in her throat.

"Are you?" she questioned.

"Of course, I would never want you to be alone. If he is where your heart truly lies, then so be it. There's no need for me to complicate matters."

He turned back to the mirror.

"Were you at the masquerade ball at Christmas?" she blurted out.

His back tensed beneath the cape. "Wouldn't I tell you if I was?" he asked.

"No," she replied. "I don't think you would. Not if you thought it would change how I thought about you."

A knock sounded on his door. When he called them to enter, Colleen and Taylor walked in.

"Oh, I'm sorry," Taylor said. "I'm here to help you change into the red suit for the masquerade."

"And I had to say... wow," Colleen said. "You are amazing."

"Thank you," he said. Then, his eyes went to Cassie. "I'll see you on stage."

"I just hope, if I had someone like the phantom watching out for me like he did for Christine or someone who hid their face from me, he would tell me how much he cared, and reveal it before it's too late."

Trevor said nothing as he stood before the mirror. Cassie felt tears prick her eyes.

My god what have I done? She wondered as she left the dressing room.

Chapter Twenty Seven

Trevor's phone chirped on the counter. His father was texting him at intermission, but Trevor did not want to check it, he could imagine his father's reaction after the initial text;

Dad: Damn, son! That was amazing, but what's going on?

Trevor: What do you mean?

Dad: The reprise... I got chills and you moved your ma and sister to tears. Not that you're not amazing, but it seemed like a lot of pain, angst, and anger went into that song and more than just acting. It looked like you were actually crying, and your voice cracked, in a good way of course, it added to the character but... What happened?

Trevor: Well, as of circle up... they're engaged.

Now, the phone chimed again, and Trevor could only imagine his dad's response. Instead of checking it, he stood before the mirror as Taylor helped him out of the outfit he wore without hurting the makeup nor the bald cap and wig. Colleen stood by the door.

"All right," Trevor sighed. "Just say it."

"Why didn't you tell her?" Colleen blurted, "That was your chance."

"Yeah, Trev, you should have told her everything. I mean I know you say there's rules about it and guys don't steal other guys' girls, which is sexist by the way, but come on."

"Ladies, thank you for your interest and Taylor, thanks for your help earlier, but there's no way I can tell her, not now."

"There is," she urged. "Tell her everything. You both deserve to hear it."

"And besides, I'm with Tay on this," Colleen said. "We aren't living in the Dark Ages nor the Victorian Era, nor any other time where women didn't have any rights. It's the twenty-first century for god sakes. She deserves the respect due to her to make her own decisions on who she wants to be with."

"I'm not trying to take her decision away," Trevor stated.

"Trying or not, you are," Taylor replied. "By not telling her the truth, you're not giving her all the information she needs to make a decision. It's like a doctor going into a surgery not knowing if someone is allergic to some sort of medicine or not. They can't make judgment calls on the surgery."

"Are you saying love is like an allergic reaction?" Trevor asked sardonically.

"Sometime," Taylor and Colleen replied together.

"Look," Colleen when on. "You can't have some sort of measuring contest and expect her to just pick whichever one wins between the two. You have to let her make the choice."

Trevor huffed. "What would you do? Or what would you want done if you were her?"

"If I cared for someone as much as you care for her? I'd tell him and let him make his choice. At least then he would have all the information to make an informed decision."

"Yeah, and if he kept his choice, then at least I knew I had done everything in my power," Colleen said. Then, looking down, she twisted her fingers. "I'd want to be given the choice with all the information needed." Her soft voice made him wonder if she'd been hurt in the past.

Trevor waited for her to look back up at him and when he caught her eye, he slowly nodded. "You're right." Then, looking at Taylor he smiled slightly. "You're both right." Rushing to his duffle bag, he pulled out his keys. "Will you help me?"

Taylor stared at the keys and then smiled. She was the only one in regular clothes, granted she wore all black as was usual for a stagehand, but it was better than Trevor's Phantom and Colleen's ballerina outfits. Grabbing the keys from him, Taylor nodded. "What can I do?" Colleen grinned, clapped her hands, and squealed excitedly.

"Go to my flat, number three off Grafton Street above the deli. This key will get you in. In the bookshelf there's an oriental box. Inside is a red, black, and gold mask. Bring it to me? I'm going to wear it at the masquerade."

"That will help her make a decision?" Taylor asked.

Trevor nodded. "I'll tell you everything later but please go. It's two minutes from campus.

"I go now. Coll, will you be able to help him change?"

"I got this, go, hurry," Colleen stated.

"Number three, oriental box, got it." Taylor raced out as Colleen walked over to him and helped him remove the cap, tuxedo, and mask without hurting the makeup.

"So be it," he said softly. This was the moment Trevor had been waiting for. The moment he revealed *he* was the man behind the mask, not Robbie. The women were right. Cassie deserved to know all the facts and he could no longer allow her to live in the dark. It was time.

Chapter Twenty Eight

Recently engaged, portraying a recently engaged woman, Cassie was beyond happy. All thought of the drama off stage, gone. Trevor would come around. He was her friend and though she was attracted to him, she was going to marry Robbie, her own live Raoul.

The music for the second act began and as she took Robbie's hand in hers, he turned to her and smiled. Yes, that was the man behind the mask. She may have had her doubts in the beginning, but she was more certain than ever.

The ensemble was dynamic and as they continued to sing *Masquerade*, Cassie's excitement grew. Soon, it was their cue and Robbie and Cassie walked on the stage singing their parts and dancing together.

Then, the music changed, indicating Trevor had stepped on the stage in his red suit and skull mask but what greeted her as she looked up the steps on the stage was the mask of the mysterious stranger from the Christmas Masquerade. Trevor stood in his full red suit, but the mask was the red, black, and gold Venetian mask of the man she fell in love with. The man she kissed, the man who promised to get her the perfume so she would know who he was.

Phantom.

Trevor.

Oh, dear god, it was him all along. He locked eyes with hers, and she read the truth in those beautiful ice blue eyes. Trevor O'Quinn was the masked man all along. She loved him. She had always loved him. She had tried to force the love she thought she was supposed to feel for Robbie, but it was nothing like the free flowing feeling she had when looking at Trevor.

Turning to Robbie, his jaw was set and when he looked at her, his eyes were hard with the same look he always had just before he struck her. The ugly truth stared at her. Robbie's grip on her hand grew painful. Not having his lies any longer, she twisted out of his hold. His eyes grew wide and promised a strong reaction as soon as they were off stage. But no, she was done paying the victim. She was done falling for his lies. Not again. He would never lay another finger on her.

Turning back to Trevor, still singing his part, she took her cue when the Phantom began speaking to Christine. She slowly walked up the steps, her back to the audience.

Soon, she and Trevor were face to face. She raised her hand, brushing her fingers across the mask, her gaze locked on Trevor's.

I didn't know, she mouthed. *I'm sorry.*

The corner of his mouth ticked up and her heart lightened. It all made sense. Everything from his subtle hints, to the perfume and roses she had on her dressing room counter that day.

Trevor was her Phantom. The smile lifting her lips, would not go away and for a second, she was back at the masquerade dancing with him. Then, a memory of another man wearing an old-fashioned doctor's mask, standing off to the side when they finished dancing. The time she asked for the perfume. That man... Robbie, eavesdropped... lied... *oh dear god. No wonder Trevor was angry.* Hating herself for ever believing Robbie was anything like the man before her.

Love, pure, complicated, and brilliant flowed through her. But soon she was pulled back to the show by the sudden music change and Trevor finishing his scene then leaving the stage in a flash. Turning back to Robbie before she raced off the opposite way, his face was hard as stone. One thing was certain, she would have a talk with him, but until then, they could not be alone together.

Trevor stepped off stage to see Taylor the stagehand who had helped him. She gave him the biggest smile and he picked her up in a hug.

"Thank you!"

"Put me down," she laughed. "Prof Lipscomb would fire me on the spot if he saw you. You could throw your back out and then what good would you be to her?" she wiggled her brows suggestively. He laughed but promptly clamped his mouth shut as he was scolded by one of the other stagehands.

He smiled again at her and hurried to change for his next scene in the cemetery after one of Cassie's solos.

Chapter Twenty Nine

Final curtain, a standing ovation and a solid five minutes of continuous applause, Cassie was beyond excited to see Trevor again. The kiss between the Phantom and Christine had been passionate, but they had to stop with the music and as soon as she was off the stage, she was going to find him and kiss him properly, not in character but as Cassie and Trevor. Her lips still tingled with the memory of their first kiss at the ball. As soon as he kissed her on stage, she recognized his touch.

Walking down the steps to the Green Room, she pulled her hair free from the bobby pins and shook it out. A smile crossed her lips as she daydreamed about Trevor but then someone grabbed her arm and wrenched her around. Robbie.

"Is that how it's going to be?" he demanded. "The Yank

dangles that mask and you're a quivering mess?"

"No, he dangles that mask and I realize how much of a liar and fraud you are, Robbie. I was actually falling in love with you, but there was always something missing. For the longest time, I thought it was me, but it was you all along. You listened in and thought you could steal me away. Then you continually lied to me. I hoped you had changed. I liked who you were the last two months but that was also a lie. You are a desperate, arrogant arse and I'm sorry I spent the time I did with you when I could have been with the man who loves me for me and who I love more than I thought possible."

Pain exploded across her face. She was stunned for a second until she realized what had happened. Robbie had swiped the back of his hand across her face. Gasping, she looked back at him to seeing the ugly look in his eyes she hadn't seen for nearly two months.

Before she could do anything more, there was a roar followed by a flurry of white shirt and black cape lunging forward, grabbing Robbie by the lapels of his costume, lifting him up, his feet dangling off the ground, then throwing him to the wall. Robbie's back struck the hard, wooden door to the costume room and he slid down to the floor. The black cape grabbed him and lifted him up. A knee to the groin and a punch across Robbie's jaw, the man who had once tormented her and then became her fiancé lay in a heap moaning on the ground.

She stared at him for a long moment, then the black cape stood before her. Looking up, Trevor breathed heavily. His face still covered in the Phantom's mask for curtain call. He gently stroked his thumb across her aching cheek. Tears pooled in her eyes as she gazed up at him.

"Did he hurt you anywhere else?" he demanded gently.

Cassie shook her head and wrapped her arms around his

middle holding him close.

"Thank you," she said.

"I'm sorry," he replied. "I saw him rear back to strike you, but I couldn't get to you fast enough."

She shook her head. "It's okay. That's the last time he ever hits me."

"Agreed," Trevor replied.

"I love you," she said softly. Pulling back, she kept her arms around him but looked deeply into his eyes. "I love you, Trevor. I hoped it was you. All this time, I wanted it to be you and it was. It's always been you."

"It was me," he said. "I told you I was going home so I could tell you how I really felt about you without fear of you rejecting me." He shrugged. "I guess I was concerned you wouldn't feel the same. Robbie overheard somehow and when I came back from Norway with your perfume, I saw him give it to you and you believed it. I couldn't tell you."

"I wish you had. I would have preferred you any day."

"You have me now, love. I'm never letting you go."

"Promise."

"Swear it, on that bottle of perfume and my mask," he replied.

Cassie could wait no longer. Pushing up to her toes, she pressed her lips to his. Trevor held her tightly to him, his lips firm and yet gentle. He teased his tongue with hers, giving and taking everything she wanted.

Only when they hear Professor Lipscomb come down the stairs, did they pull back and look around them. The other actors were staring.

Lipscomb's eyes went from Cassie and Trevor to Robbie still sobbing on the ground, holding himself as pain from Trevor's knee must still be radiating.

"All right... what happened here?" Lipscomb asked.

"I'm sorry, professor. It's a long story," Cassie replied.

"Short version, sir," Trevor started. "Robbie is a predator and has hurt Cassie many times in the past. She was trapped and had to accept his proposal earlier tonight because if she didn't, he would hurt her again."

"Lies! I would never," Robbie whimpered.

"It's true. I saw him hit her," Colleen stepped forward.

"When I saw him hit her, I defended her." Trevor shrugged.

"It's true, da'," Trevor turned to see Taylor standing on the other side of Meg. "I saw the whole thing and I've noticed the bruises on Cassie's wrist before. She's been my study-buddy for this session. Tutoring me in maths."

Lipscomb nodded slowly.

"Wait... dad?" Trevor questioned looking between Lipscomb and Taylor.

She smiled. "Yeah, Prof is my dad."

"But I thought..." Trevor cut off.

Lipscomb raised an eyebrow. "You thought what?"

Trevor took in his light pink button up shirt and paisley tie. "Nothing," Trevor shook his head. "But I promise that is what happened. I was trying to protect Cassie."

"Well then, best change and go out to greet your fans. You won't have to worry about Mr. McConaghy. He will be struck from the show," Lipscomb promised. Turning to his daughter, he continued. "Let's have new inserts printed up for the program." Taylor nodded and typed something into her phone.

"You can't do that!" Robbie cried.

"I can," Lipscomb stated. "And I have. I think Young Mr. Evans would be an excellent choice," he turned to the second-year student.

"I would love to, sir," Mr. Evans said. "Thank you!"

"Good, I'll need all three of you here around one tomorrow to make sure we give Mr. Evans the best chance possible. And Mr. Evans, I will need you here at ten am sharp to go over your lines and songs. I believe for tomorrow's performance I will make an announcement to the audience that you will be using the libretto for some scenes as Raoul's part can be complicated and I don't want you to push yourself."

"Thank you, sir, I will do my best," Evans stated.

"You can't do that!" Robbie cried again, slowly standing. "Do you have any idea who my father is? He'll have your job!"

"I know Collin McConaghy well," Lipscomb replied. "We were friends in university. I'm sure he would take a particular dislike to how you have treated Miss Doyle. I will be speaking with him tonight."

"No! You can't," Robbie tried again then, with a sort of rage in his eyes, he raced to Trevor.

Trevor pushed Cassie behind him and took a stance. Robbie reared back, his fist tight. Trevor met his fist with an open hand, held Robbie's punch and, using Robbie's momentum, he pushed him back. Robbie stumbled and failed to get his feet back under him. Falling on his arse, he cried out in anger and frustration. Cassie couldn't help but laugh a bit hysterically. He looked so little compared to Trevor's six-foot two-inch muscular frame.

Robbie got back to his feet, but Lipscomb stepped between them. "Attack him again, and I will call the Garda." Robbie thought better of it and looked down. Lipscomb turned to his daughter, "Tay, go get your brothers. I'll need them to escort Mr. McConaghy out."

"Okay, da'." Taylor grinned as she passed Trevor and Cassie. "It's amazing when people get their comeuppance."

Without another word, she hurried up the stairs. Lipscomb looked at two other actors in the troupe and nodded. They stepped forward to watch Robbie as the professor looked back at Trevor and Cassie.

"I wanted to tell you, you both have been asked to meet a Julie Richardson in the VIP bar lounge in twenty minutes."

"Who is that?" Cassie asked.

"I won't spoil it, but I know you will be excited to hear what she has to say," he winked and made a shooing motion with his hand. "Oh, Miss Doyle," he called her back. "I hope you know this," he motioned to Robbie. "Will no longer be an issue for you. I wish you to know, I am sorry for the abuse you suffered while under my protection. I hope you know you can always come to me and talk if you need help or advice."

"Thank you, Professor," she replied.

"No thanks needed," he said. "I hope my daughter will find someone who cares for her as much as Mr. O'Quinn cares for you." Then, he grinned and turned to Trevor. "Have any brothers?"

Trevor laughed. "One, but he's sixteen so..." Lipscomb debated. "But I have plenty of cousins."

"That'll do," he winked. "Now, get you gone and take that makeup off."

Chapter Thirty

Trevor and Cassie hurriedly got changed and Trevor pulled off the Phantom's makeup, grateful he still had eyebrows by the time they were done. He met Cassie at the stairs going up to the lobby. The moment they reached the main cast door, Trevor stopped and looked down at her. Taking her hand in his, he kissed her fingers.

"Before we go, I need to tell you something," he said.

"What?" She asked.

"I lied to you when I said I was going home before the Masquerade. I was scared, you see."

"Scared?"

"Yeah," he breathed. "I was in love with you, Cassie and it seemed you only wanted me as a friend which I thought I was okay with, but... I wasn't. I was scared if I came right out and said how I felt I'd lose you as a friend too and I couldn't bare that. So, I came up with a plan. Be intriguing to you. Wear the mask, channel my father's voice, he's deeper and more accented than mine, and tell you that way."

"So very theatrical, phantom," she teased.

"Heh," he chuckled. "Yeah, I guess. I wanted to tell you so many times, but there was always Robbie standing in our way. There's this sort of unspoken rule between guys. You seemed happy so I left well enough alone. Then we didn't have any classes together this session. But when I saw those bruises on your wrist and saw how he manhandled you, I knew I had to help. I'm no knight in shining armor and you don't ever have to be with me because I might have protected you from him. You owe me nothing, I want you to want to be with me because you want to be with me. Not because you feel like you have to. Was that sexist? That sounded sexist. I didn't mean it. I'm tongue-tied. I'm sorry."

She grinned and cupped his jaw. "Hey, I know you're not a knight in shining armor, I had my choice and if I didn't want you or Robbie, I wouldn't be with you or Robbie. But every girl dreams of a sexy knight or a redheaded Viking warrior whisking her off to his castle and loving her. At least, most of the women I know have told me they share the same dream. I care about you, Trevor. And I choose you. I always wanted it to be you."

He smiled and stroked her cheek. "Love you too."

"What?"

"You just basically said you loved me."

"No, I didn't," she giggled.

"Sure you did," winking he wrapped his arms around her.

"I'm glad you're the first one to say it."

"Keep dreaming, O'Quinn," her cheeks hurt from smiling too much.

After a beat, his grin softened, and he leaned his forehead against hers. "I do love you, Cassie Doyle. I always have. You spoiled me for all other women."

"Flattering but hopefully untrue, Trevor," she said. "I didn't mean to."

"I know you didn't mean to, woman. But it's true. And I've done some things recently that I'm not a fan of, but it's over now and my heart is as always yours."

"Mine is and always will be yours, Trevor," she kissed him then. Their lips meeting in a flash and though passion ran through them both, the kiss was more exploratory than hurried. They took their time, learning and memorizing each other's moves, likes, and feel. It was no where near Trevor's first kiss, but it was by far his favorite. Her taste exploded on his tongue as he teased her lips apart and dived in. Groaning slightly when he felt her pull even closer to him, their bodies flushed against each other. Finally, they pulled apart, panting, and staring at each other.

"You are so beautiful," he breathed, taking in her flushed face and dilated eyes. She smiled but didn't speak, her chest heaving with their kiss. "Go out with me? I want to take you out on a date."

"Yes," she answered without hesitation. "When?"

"Tomorrow night?"

She groaned. "Monday? This show is going to take so much out of me this weekend and with everything I need a day to recover."

"Monday it is then," he agreed. Kissing her lightly once

more, he nuzzled her nose with his and glanced at the closed door. "We should probably get out there."

"Yeah," she stated. "Oh god, what am I going to tell my family?"

"The truth?" He offered. "I'm sure they know a little already."

"Padraig figured it out, you said."

"Yeah, he asked me pointblank and I couldn't lie but I didn't divulge anything but my omittance, he took as agreement. I'm sorry, Cassie. It wasn't my place to say anything."

"And you didn't. Padraig is very perceptive. He reads people very well. It's okay. I'm kind of glad, makes it easier."

"I'll be with you if you want. I can provide moral support."

"I'll always want you with me," she kissed him briefly, just a brush of her lips against his.

"We should go," Trevor said.

"Yeah, promise me one thing."

"Anything?"

"You'll never lose that mask."

Trevor barked a laugh. "I promise, love. I may even find... unique times to wear it."

She giggled but soon they pushed open the door and walked out into the lobby. The gathered crowd of VIP audience members broke into applause. Trevor looked around at mainly the cast and crew's family members, but what caught his eye was the location. Six months ago, he stood at the base of the stairs wearing a black suit jacket, tuxedo pants, a white button up shirt, not buttoned all the way and his Venetian mask, waiting for Cassie

197

to arrive. It felt like only a day ago, he had debated on tie, bowtie, or no tie, but he remembered seeing her at the top of the red carpeted stairs in her red dress and swan mask. He stopped and looked down at her. Cassie's eyes met his.

"I wanted to do this again right here where it all began," he said. Her smile widened and she nodded. He leaned down and pressed his lips to hers as the audience gasped and cheered.

When they pulled back, Trevor caught his father's eye, a grin split his face. Emmet raised a glass of champagne toward him and winked. Mara stood with Cassie's mom and they both had happy tears in their eyes. But soon Trevor looked toward the VIP bar lounge and a woman with short blonde hair was watching them.

"I think we should go say hello to our parents, but we need to meet Julie."

"I think our parents would understand. Let's meet with her now. I don't want to keep her waiting. Whatever and whoever she is, Lipscomb seemed happy for us," Cassie said.

Trevor agreed and found his father's gaze once more. Motioning that they'd be right over in two minutes, Emmet nodded and turned to relay the message to the others. Trevor did see his American Aunt and Uncle had made the trip again to see him. But then he saw his cousin Peter and beside him was his friend Geoffrey Ainsley. Trevor waved at them both, it had been almost a year since he had seen Geoff and always like talking to the former Special Reconnaissance Regiment Unit Commander of the British Army.

Cassie and Trevor made their way slowly through the crowd. People stopped them and told them how marvelous they were. With thanks, they said they'll be right back and had someone who asked for a meeting but to please stay for the champagne toast that always happened on Opening and Closing Night as a celebration.

Ms. Richardson was waiting patiently by the entrance to the VIP lounge, a fresh martini in her hand.

"Ms. Richardson?" Trevor questioned. "We apologize for being tardy."

"I expected it, Mr. O'Quinn and please call me Julie," she said. "You have many fans who wanted to say hello. I happen to be one of them as well. An excellent performance. One of the best I have seen colleges put on."

"Thank you, do I detect a Midwestern accent?" Trevor asked.

"You do indeed," she answered. "Born and raised in Cincinnati."

"I grew up not far from there. Indianapolis," Trevor said. "And Cassie's mum is American."

"From Boston," Cassie supplied.

"Interesting," Julie replied, absently tapping her acrylic nails on the stem of the glass. "Well, I won't keep you long, but I wanted to offer my services."

"Your services?" Trevor questioned.

"Yes, I know you both recently graduated, and I was wondering if you had thought of grad school."

"We both have thought of it," Cassie answered. "I have applied to some but haven't heard back."

"Not uncommon," Julie encouraged. "I am a recruiter... a broker of sorts. I find the talent and get them placed into the correct college. I help make it an easy transition. I also am the main point of contact for both you and the university, so you are not bombarded with unanswerable emails."

"Interesting, what is your fee?" Trevor asked.

Julie raised a single eyebrow. "Financial, I'm impressed." Trevor said nothing and waited. "I am paid through the school on retainer. My clients, you, would not pay out of pocket. I take on a few select clients and I would like to speak with you both further. Could we have coffee tomorrow?"

"I should tell you, Julie," Cassie started. "My family are not well off. I was here on scholarship. I would not be able to go to grad school unless I had a full ride scholarship or at least an eighty percent one."

"Doable, with your voice and talent," Julie answered.

Trevor looked to Cassie, his entire body humming with excitement. From her deathlike grip on his hand and mile wide grin on her face, she must feel it too.

"Then, I would be extremely interested in speaking with you. We are needed here at one o'clock tomorrow would nine be too early?" Cassie asked.

"Nine would be fine," Julie replied. "Let me give you my number and we can meet at the coffee shop directly across from the university."

"That would be grand," Trevor pulled out his phone and programmed her number. "Thank you, Julie, we are looking forward to seeing you tomorrow. Please stay for the champagne toast."

"Oh, thank you," she answered. "I didn't know they were doing that."

Trevor snagged two glasses off a passing waiter and handed one to Julie and one to Cassie. The waiter waited for him to grab another and then passed the audience members still waiting. After a quick goodbye, Trevor and Cassie took their drink and made their way to their family.

After what felt like an hour, they finally reached them. Cassie mother grabbed her to her and hugged her tightly. Emmet pulled Trevor into a strong embrace and thumped his back.

"So proud of you," Emmet said. "So damn proud."

"Em, language," Mara tsked but soon pulled Trevor into a hug too. "So proud of you, sweetie, but what happened?" she whispered. "Your last text to your dad was they were engaged."

"Long story," Trevor replied.

"Tell me later," Mara smiled and cupped his jaw.

"Trevor? I'd like you meet my dad," Cassie said. Trevor nodded and headed her way. Once introductions were made all around, Lipscomb took his place at the top of the stairs and clinked a silver knife to his champagne glass. A hush descended and Emmet walked up next to his son.

"I made reservations at The Castle Restaurant. We sat next to Cassie's family and when I saw you wearing the mask, I realized what you were doing," Emmet said. Trevor side-glanced toward his dad to see the smirk playing on his lips. "I called just now to expand our reservations inviting Cassie's family."

"I would love that, but I don't think they can afford it, dad," Trevor whispered. "Castle is pretty expensive."

"I made it clear I wanted to do this for us to get to know each other. Her father and I had a conversation," Emmet explained. "He offered to buy a couple bottles of wine for us, I didn't want to insult the man, so I agreed."

"Have I told you how amazing you are, dad?" Trevor asked. Emmet looked over at him, his brows furrowed. "I love you. Thank you. You are the best dad in the world."

Tears gathered in the corner of Emmet's eyes, but he patted his son's shoulder and pulled him into an awkward side hug. "I love you too, son," he added as he kissed his son's temple. Trevor laughed and lovingly pushed him away.

Lipscomb's attention was drawn to Trevor who grimaced and waved an apology.

"I wanted to thank everyone for coming tonight and for staying to greet our two leads. Unfortunately, Robbie McConaghy, our Raoul has been detained and unable to join us. He has been removed from this production for personal reasons and replaced by a young man who joined us tonight as Monsieur Lefèvre and *his* part will be played by one of our highly accomplished ensemble members. It has been an exciting six months. At Christmas time, we held a masquerade ball right here in this very spot. It was also where we first noticed our leads and embarrassing them again tonight, where we saw their chemistry." Trevor chuckled and looked over at Cassie. Her cheeks were a soft pink and she looked down. "Now, is everyone served?" At the general sound of agreement, Lipscomb continued. "As is tradition, we all join in a champagne toast congratulating our stars and wishing the production well as it continues for another two weekends. Sláinte!" He raised his glass in a toast. Trevor looked over at Cassie and raised his toward her with a wink. She smiled and did the same.

The fresh taste of bubbling champagne hit his taste buds and he closed his eyes. He could hardly believe how everything turned out. He stood in the same location where his life took a turn six months ago and again it changed for the best. Cassie was near to him, his own even, and he had the role of his dreams. He graduated with honors from the university he always wanted to attend, and he had his family near him. Taking a deep breath, he raised his eyes and his glass to the heavens.

"Thank you, mom," he whispered. "Miss you."

Emmet squeezed his shoulder in comfort. "She would be so proud of you."

Trevor nodded and looked at his dad. "Thank you, dad. For everything."

"I am so proud and excited for you, Trev. I know whatever happens next will be an adventure with Cassie by your side."

Trevor agreed and as he caught Cassie's wink, he smiled. His character was right, she was his *angel of music* and he was very much looking forward to the future with her.

Epilogue

Two years later – Indianapolis

Cassie rolled over as the early sunlight streamed through the windows of their small bungalow just off College Avenue and sixty-second street, to see her husband seated at his desk, going over some paperwork.

"What steals you from our bed before coffee?" she asked after watching for a long moment.

He looked up with a smile and stood. Walking over to her, he crawled into bed beside her.

"Paperwork Julie wants me to finish before my exam," he explained after greeting her with a good morning kiss.

"Tell our school broker to leave you alone for ten minutes. It's Saturday and your wife wants you."

"My wife had me all night," he replied kissing her chest just above the swell of his favorite curves.

"So? There's no limit to her need." She stroked her fingers through his hair.

Trevor chuckled and moved up to her neck to give a kiss, suck, and nip. Pulling back, he was satisfied with the growing hickey.

"You know full well, my love the excuse of you needing me hasn't worked on her since we were newlyweds a year ago," Trevor teased.

"Then tell her, I am in need of your extra special attention."

"I'd rather not tell her about our sex life," he winked. She giggled.

"Poor Julie," she said. "She probably wouldn't know what to do with that information, especially if you happen to mention what you do with that mask..."

Trevor laughed and wiggled his eyebrows suggestively then proceeded to kiss her, moving his way down further.

"After our graduation," he began between kisses, "I am all yours, love. And you are all mine." He punctuated each of his words with a kiss. "I was thinking we could go back to Norway to that little town we love. Or maybe Venice for the wine and cheese festival?"

"Oh yeah, when is that?"

"September," he announced.

"Yes, please," she replied.

"I'll work on tickets," he said. "Da' was also asking us to come home for Aiofe's and Killian's graduation."

"Did he finally tell your parents he wasn't going to college?"

"He told them he wasn't sure, but I think he's looking at a trade schools," Trevor admitted, falling to her side on the bed and pulling her to rest against him. "Maybe not a four-year degree but something. He's always tinkering with our cars, so maybe he'll take after our Uncle Tom and be a mechanic."

"That would be a great job for him," she agreed.

"He'd enjoy it," Trevor replied absently stroking her exposed back.

Cassie's phone chirped an email notification on the nightstand and Trevor reached over to grab it and hand it to her. She smiled when she saw a text from her brother. Every morning they would text each other but, ignoring the email she just received, she stared at the text. It was sent late last night after she and Trevor had gone on to bed which meant it was just dawn back in Ireland. Though it wasn't unusual for her brother to be up before the sun as he helped their dad around the farm, but what made her pause was the link he sent to a newspaper article.

"Everything okay?" Trevor asked and she breathed out.

"Listen to this," she started and began reading. "'Scandal at McConaghy Whiskey. Sources close to the power couple Irene and Collin McConaghy have confirmed, after an arduous two-year divorce case, the separation and dissolution of marriage has been granted. A clause in the prenuptial agreement allowed Mr. McConaghy to file for divorce after all their children had graduated from university. Though the proceedings started two years ago, Mrs. McConaghy, it is said was not going peacefully and wanted a percentage of the whiskey distillery. The scene that erupted inside the courtroom was nothing short of intense. Mrs. McConaghy, it is said, was arrested for assaulting her husband and barrister when the judge settled for her husband's counter offer of giving her the house and one million euros instead of the ten million, she demanded. Both her husband and her barrister are said to be fine. Outside the courthouse, this paper caught up with their eldest son and his wife for a statement. Though Charles McConaghy is now sole owner of McConaghy Whiskey, it is said he still reaches out to his brother who is serving eleven months for funneling company funds into his personal account. Charles McConaghy had this to say'..." her voice trailed off.

"Robbie in jail?" Trevor questioned.

"Apparently," she breathed.

"Honestly, baby, can't say I'm surprised. His temper? I'm just amazed it wasn't a pub fight or something," Trevor stated.

"Yeah," she murmured.

"Hey, you okay?"

She looked up at him. "Of course, sorry, it's just pretty shocking. The man I was going to spend the rest of my life with is in jail."

"Thank providence you aren't spending your life with him, then," Trevor grinned. She beamed up at him.

"I always do," she answered.

"It's still shocking, love, I know," Trevor kissed her forehead. "I don't mean to make light of it."

A giggle burst from her lips and Trevor stared at her for a long moment. Another giggle and then another.

"Ehm..." Trevor started.

She waved him off as she kept laughing and tears ran down his face. "It's just... he tormented me for so long and now he's in jail... I don't know, I just found that awfully funny." She calmed and kissed her husband. "Thank you for putting up with my quirkiness."

"I love your quirkiness," he winked and kissed her softly.

"I was thinking," she began after a few moments of silence. All thought of Robbie and McConaghy Whiskey gone.

"Should I be worried?" he teased. She playfully smacked his stomach. He grunted but chuckled. "What were you thinking, love?"

"Let's go to Venice in September absolutely but anything before that might need to wait."

"Why?"

"Well," she leaned up and looked down at him. "You know how I'm working with the musical theater production department head?"

"Yeah," he answered.

"Well, I found out what production they're doing this year. They haven't announced it yet, so you are under strict secrecy."

"Scouts honor," he answered. "What's the production?"

"*Love Never Dies.*"

Trevor barked a laugh. "Seriously?" She nodded. "Interesting. I've only seen it once. It's an intriguing sequel to *Phantom of the Opera.*"

She walked her fingers up his torso. "I was thinking... maybe we could audition."

"Have a rematch as Phantom and Christine?" He asked. She nodded. Trevor raised an eyebrow. "It's sad though. Sure that won't made bad memories?"

"No," she shook her head. "And I want to sing Phantom and Christine with you again."

Trevor watched her and saw the hopeful look in her eyes. "All right, love, all right. Let's do it. Hopefully, they'll cast us correctly."

She giggled. "I won't accept if you aren't my phantom."

"Same here, darling."

"You are always my phantom. No one else will ever play opposite me in that."

He grinned. "You will always be my Christine."

She smiled and placed a kiss on his chest. "And after that, I want to go back to Dublin. I miss our families."

"*In Dublin Fair City, where the girls are so pretty,*" Trevor began to sing, smiling as he heard her words. She beamed, then squealed when he flipped her and hovered over her. Still singing as he kissed her, he had her quivering beneath him in no time.

"I love you, Trevor," she stated. He looked up at her, his icy blue eyes, glassy and dilated with anticipated pleasure and warm with love.

"I love you too, my wife, my Cassie, my *angel of music.* I love you."

Soon, they forgot everything else and throughout that Saturday, he proved just how much he loved her and how excited he was to star opposite her again, that time in the sequel to the story that shaped their lives.

an deireadh

Acknowledgements

Thank you so much for reading! I am so excited to share Trevor and Cassie with you all. Ever since I was a little girl, I have loved the *Phantom of the Opera.* In fact, the story Cassie told Trevor about her love of the tale is my own personal one. My mother introduced it to me, and we used to watch every version of the musical or book-based miniseries. It was the miniseries starring Charles Dance that made me fall in love with characters. The story behind Cassie's love of *Faust* comes from that show. When I was about twelve, I watched it and as I was an aspiring singer, I learned *Oui c'est moi J't'aime* just so I could warmup to a song from the movie.

I had just finished Emmet's book *Across the Irish Sea* where you first meet Trevor as a little boy, and I was taking a moment to enjoy wrapping up that story, when I heard a little nudge from Trevor (yes, my characters speak to me) asking me to tell his story and the first scene that came to me was when he and Cassie sing the title song at his jury. It seemed only natural to have a little of my own story associated with it. I was fortunate enough to play Christine in my Final Year Showcase in High School. It was a dream come true!

Thank you all and I hope you check back for the next book in this series: *Love Among the Shamrocks Collection The Next Generation: Song of Heart's Desire.* Set five years after *In Dublin Fair City,* we learn more about Trevor's cousin, Lachlan O'Quinn and his heartbreaking past. You will also find out the true relationship of Peter Carlisle and Peter's friend, Geoffrey Ainsley, and how war, pain, and loss united them. Lachlan's story was a joy to write! Read on for a sneak peek. Until then, please follow me on social media under the handles Author M. Katherine Clark and check out my website www.mkatherineclark.net for more information!

love among the shamrocks collection

the next generation

Book Two

The Song of
Heart's Desire

M. KATHERINE CLARK

Prologue

Saying goodbye to someone you've known and loved for over a decade was one thing. But saying goodbye to a life cut short and one you never got a chance to see? That was something entirely different.

As Lachlan O'Quinn stared down at the freshly dug grave and the casket containing his wife and stillborn daughter being lowered into the open earth, he felt the last thread of his will to live, cut clean. The smell of petrichor, fresh earth before the rain, burned his nostrils and the tears he had shed, refused to stop. They had tried so long to have a child. He and his Karin. It wasn't fair he never even got the chance to see his beautiful daughter's eyes.

Unsure if he would ever be able to forgive the teenager who had caused the car accident simply to answer a text on his phone, Lachlan kept his eyes down, focused on the grave and his anger hidden from his family who surrounded him.

But as soon as the music started, he wasn't sure he would survive. All the emotions raged within him and nothing could stop it. Falling to his knees as his muscles gave out, he reached toward the shimmering brown casket that held his heart and soul. As it was being lowered, he hoped the earth would swallow him up and he could be with his two favorite people in the world. The ground was coming closer and though tears rained down his cheeks, he didn't care. The pain was too much. He felt as if someone was cutting his chest open and scooping out his heart with a teaspoon.

Just as he thought he would get his wish, a strong hand landed on his shoulder and pulled him back. Someone screamed but only after the sound echoed, did he realize it was him. His father's arms came around him as Cabhan knelt beside him. He held him close but even a father's love and support could not end the heartache. Lachlan wept into his father's shoulder as the first of the dirt was tossed into the grave.

Cabhan pulled back and stared into his son's eyes, the same toffee color mirrored his pain. But his father wouldn't understand, he couldn't understand. He never lost his wife or a child. They all stood near him that morning. But as much as his father tried to help, nothing would be able to block out the pain of seeing his wife lying on the emergency C-section table, face bloody, eyes closed, and hearing no cry from their child as she was ripped from her mother's body. Nothing could stop it. Nothing but death and he welcomed it. Wished for it. Hoped it would swallow him up just as the earth was swallowing the only good thing to ever happen to him.

Chapter One

Ten Years Later

D r. Lachlan O'Quinn looked around the mostly empty office of his veterinarian practice in Dublin, Ireland. The last nine years in the small, but booming practice were some of the hardest of his life. But seeing it empty tugged at memories of emotions he no longer claimed to have. Turning when his secretary sighed loudly beside him, he took in his cousin's profile. Egan McArdle turned to him.

"Are you sure about this, Lach?" He asked. Being a cousin on his mother's side, Lachlan turned a deaf ear when he called him by the family nickname when they were alone. That, and he owed his cousin a lot over the years.

After his wife Karin died, Lachlan lacked purpose and drive to do anything. Egan negotiated a lease on a set of small offices on the outskirts of Dublin and nearly forced his signature on the document. Since moving from Kerry to Dublin town, Lachlan successfully buried the worst of the pain and continued living... though *living* was too strong a word for the half-life he maintained. Stashing away his emotions made him much more methodical and, in some cases, more like a machine than a human. Lachlan lived every day waiting for the morning he could rejoin his wife.

Still, the idea of moving back home, stirred his heart more than he was willing to admit.

"I'm sure," he stated. "Da's retiring and there's no one to take over. I'm the logical one"

"Logical," Egan shook his head and sighed again, placing his hands on his slim hips. "All right, Spock. What else needs to be done?"

"Everything in the moving van?" Lachlan asked.

"Yep," he answered. "Perfectly packed as per your instructions."

"Good," Lachlan nodded. "How about the flat?"

"That team, led by your brother, is already on their way to Killarney. He wanted you to head over before you left and check it out. Also, give final keys."

Lachlan dug in his pocket. Offering Egan the keys to his flat, he locked eyes with him.

"I'd rather not go back," he said. "It's hard enough leaving here."

Egan nodded and took the keys.

With one more look around, he refused to feel the stirrings of sadness in his chest. Nearly ten years, the office on Grange Road near the National Park, was his home away from home. The one good thing about his solitude, was the ability to meet his cousins Trevor or Egan for lunch or sometimes supper when Trevor was studying at Trinity University. But since he graduated five years ago and moved with his wife to America, they hadn't stayed as close as before which saddened him… if he could *feel* sad.

Having Trevor and his other family, his Uncle Innis' family, less than twenty minutes away was a lifeline to his self-preservation and prevented him from ending at all. Too many times he had come in early, gone straight to the tranquilizers, grabbed a syringe, and nearly ended his life, but the thought of his family stopped him and once, his Uncle Innis had walked in, just as Lachlan held the syringe to his skin. The shock then look of determination reflected in his uncle's eyes haunted Lachlan. Since then, Innis had made sure to call him and set him up with a counselor. Talking about the loss had helped him put the desire of self-harm away but it never fully left the back of his mind. The only thing that helped him, was work. Animals never let him down and they never got too close to his heart.

"Lach, I'm gonna ask you one more time. Are you sure about this?" Egan questioned. "Because it's not too late. You can tell Dr. Harris you aren't moving out."

"The lease is already switched," he shook his head. "Besides, I couldn't do that to my da' or my brother."

His baby brother was thirteen years younger than him. At twenty-five, Oisín had started his own moving company and it was quite the hit with the ladies of all ages because the movers had to be buff young men, willing to wear nothing but a kilt and boots, a remnant of when he had studied in Scotland.

Not caring what the old biddies, or young women in his complex thought about the men moving his things, Lachlan only wanted to help his brother's business but refused to be in the same location as the *Rough and Buff* movers. There was a lot he'd do for his little brother but seeing him and his college buddies shirtless and in a kilt was not one of them.

"I'm driving straight through tonight," Lachlan stated. "I should be there directly after them, so I'll go to the office first. They know to set that up before the cottage, right?"

"It's in the notes," Egan replied. "Whether or not they read is another issue."

Lachlan gave him his usual blank look. His cousin may have been only thirty-two, but he was as ornery and cantankerous about the younger generation as any seventy-year-old.

"Well, since there's no convincing you otherwise, I'll just say I'm going to miss you, ya old goat," he said.

"Don't start that," Lachlan replied. He was already feeling the creeping fingers of sadness tickle his belly and, as with any emotion, he pushed it firmly away.

Egan cleared his throat and looked away. "Still, you're family."

"Kerry is four hours away."

"Aye, but who do I call now when I want a pint and don't want to drink alone?"

Lachlan allowed the corner of his mouth to tick up.

"Well, there is this novel idea of getting friends."

"Ah, friends are overrated," he waved him off. Lachlan scoffed, the closest thing to a chuckle he'd done in a decade. If he was going to be perfectly frank, he was going to miss him too.

Clearing his own throat, he offered a goodbye embrace. They clung to each other and thumped the other's back.

"I'm gonna miss you," Lachlan said, surprised by the emotion welling in his chest. Egan had been there. He had been there when Lachlan worked himself nearly to death. He had been there when Lachlan drank himself into an oblivion on the five year anniversary and he had been there when Lachlan cut off all emotion and still, he teased him, was there for him, helped him see he had reason for still being on earth and now he was leaving that all behind.

He tightened his embrace on his cousin and then let him go. Holding a hand to his shoulder, he stood arm's length away from him. Only then did he realize, for all his fluff and fuddle, Egan McArdle was his best friend. Or as close to a best friend as he allowed himself to have.

A breath in, as deep as he had ever been able to take since his wife died, he squeezed his cousin's shoulder and nodded to him.

"Ah, get on the road," Egan huffed. "Call me if you get tired."

"I will," Lachlan promised. "Thank you again. For everything."

"You're welcome," Egan said. "Tell your mom, my auntie, I love her when you see her."

Lachlan promised he would and, not wanting to draw out their goodbye any longer, he grabbed his medical bag, personal duffel bag, he knew he would be living out of until he could unpack, and took his car keys. One final look around the office, he let Egan out, and shut and locked the door.

Not one for hyperbole, but it felt as if he was shutting the door on his life the last few years. He had started there as a new vet nine years ago, not wanting to stay in Kerry. He had left with no plan, barely any money, and a hole in his chest where his heart used to be. Traveling to Dublin on the last tank of gas he could afford and a picnic lunch his mother had packed for him, he had nowhere to go. Fortunately, his Uncle Innis, his father's brother had taken him in but there was only so long he could stay there with all his younger cousins.

Egan helped him find a place and though it wasn't far from his family the silence was golden and on some particularly bad days it was deafening.

He had done what he could to survive, not because he wanted to, but because his self-preservation prevented him from taking his own life, always reminding him of his wife's final words to him.

"You know how much I love you and how I can always rely on you to see the future where I can't."

Of course, she had said them teasingly after he had told her, after their first child was born, he saw about five more and a cottage in the countryside overlooking the Atlantic Ocean.

That never happened, of course and he left Kerry. He hadn't been back in years. He hadn't seen Karin's name on the headstone. He couldn't. That made him weak, but he didn't care.

As he sat in Dublin rush hour traffic, his gaze was pulled to the piece of metal wrapped around his finger. The gold glinted off the sun as it played peekaboo with the clouds.

He never thought he would be a widower at only twenty-eight, but he was. Now at thirty-eight, he had devoted his life to taking care of animals and the only human interactions he had, was the worried owners who wanted to make sure he was the best, which he was. Or the occasional pint he would have with one or other of his family members.

All other times, he was alone.

All because some stupid kid thought answering a text was more important than keeping his eyes on the road. *He* walked away, but his wife never walked anywhere again. The usual pain that came with the memories welled as he stared at the wedding band. He hadn't taken it off. He never would. Karin was everything to him. He loved her since they were sixteen, married her at eighteen and never saw her again at twenty-eight.

Someone honked and he looked up, the cars in front of him had moved and he was holding up the line.

With a wave to the car behind him, he pulled forward. Breaking through the heavy traffic, he was finally on the road, going home with all the memories that came with it, but starting his life over.

Chapter Two

Corinne McDonnagh stared at her father in disbelief. "You did what?" She demanded.

Her father looked down and twisted his fingers, a telltale sign he wasn't teasing.

"I'm so sorry, love," he was serious. "I didn't... He tricked me. Made me not know what I was saying."

"No, dad, that was the *Johnny Walker*. How could you?" She demanded. "The house, the car, hell, even your business, I understand but... me?"

Again, he looked away. His stocky five-foot seven-inch

frame shuddered.

"He's always wanted you," he shrugged.

"And that gives you the right to gamble me away?" Her voice took on a shrill tone.

Callum McDonnagh had a problem. A problem with cards and drink. It had already cost more than Corinne was willing to forgive but his latest was over the line.

"You gambled me, and you lost," she summarized. "So now, you expect me to roll over and allow that... That..."

How do you describe the heir of the mob in London? Anthony Rossi, the son of Ricardo Rossi, the known Italian mobster, was a slick haired, porn 'stache, smarmy thirty year old, who sported aviator sunglasses even at night, and a suit that cost more than a year's worth of her wages as a vet tech. She'd seen him. Once, at a not for profit gala for the Humane Society where she volunteered. The Rossi's were the greatest donor.

Humane. Yeah right.

She suppressed a shudder when she remembered his golden eyed gaze from across the room. He had sauntered over to her as she stood beside the board chairman and asked why *she* wasn't on the silent auction roster. The chairman gave a nervous chuckle but did nothing to defend her. That was the story of her life when it came to men. Her father, her ex-boyfriend, her primary school friend, they all let her down and never defended her. There was only one man who took care to always be there, and she stopped a smile when she remembered him swooping in, wrapping an arm around her waist, and reminding her she owed him a dance.

Geoffrey Ainsley had always been there for her. If only they were attracted to each other and he wasn't such a great friend, they would have been married by then.

Her focus back on her father, she stared at his pleading eyes. Was that the look he always gave her mother after losing everything? Was that why her body finally gave out and she died? Corinne hardened her features as every time she thought of her mother, tears pricked her eyes.

"I'm so sorry, Corrie," he said. "But he'll kill me."

"And what about me?" she demanded.

"It's only a trial marriage. You be out of it in five years," he tried to make it sound like five years was nothing. And honestly, at twenty-eight, five years wouldn't be horrible but five years with him? Never. She'd be dead before that and she be damned if she didn't fight.

She shook her head. Her father's face fell. "You condemn me to death."

"You condemned me to a fate worse than death."

"Corrie—"

"No, no, it's over, Dad. I've forgiven a lot of things as you well know, but this is beyond anything I can forgive. How could you?" She held up a hand when he opened his mouth to speak. "No, no, on second thought, don't answer that. There's nothing you could say to make this remotely better." She grabbed her purse and phone.

"Where are you going?" he questioned.

"It's better you don't know. Wouldn't want you to gamble that away, too."

"Don't contact me. Don't try to find me."

"Corrie!"

She slammed the door as she left.

Chapter Three

Lachlan ran his hand across Donovan's flank and down his chestnut leg. The horse whinnied and pawed deep gashes in the dirt.

"What seems to be the problem?" Lachlan asked Old Widow McKeel who stood at the entrance of the horse barn.

"Problem?" she questioned.

"With Donovan," he said indicating the horse.

"Oh, well, he's just not himself," she replied.

Lachlan suppressed his groan. Since arriving back in Kerry County, he had been called out nearly every week to multiple farms and had many visits to his father's – *his* office – and all were the same reasoning. But what was annoying was, each one was widowed women, or those who had single daughters or granddaughters who conveniently showed up while he was there and invited to tea simply to be set up with him.

Sure enough, he turned to look at her, her eyes were glued to his arse.

The woman was older but did not deserve the nickname of *Old Widow McKeel.* She was a blushing young bride forty years ago when, at twenty-two, she married Farmer McKeel, a man twice widowed but the wealthiest farmer in the county. When McKeel died, she became the most notorious widow. A *wealthy cougar* was the most talked about and apparently, she set her sights on Lachlan... or rather, his arse.

"Well," he gently patted the horse's side. "Looks like he's all right now, so he is. If something else happens, give me a call." He gathered his things.

"It's not just the horse," she stepped forward. He froze. "I've been feeling poorly too."

What was this a cheap movie? Where are the cameras? He thought. "Sorry to hear that. Doc Needlers just moved in down the street. I'll send him over."

Standing, he nodded in her direction and walked sternly to the barn door.

"Don't you want to help me?" Her voice came out sounding husky. Lachlan sighed.

It had happened before. Not with her, but others. He'd been told he was attractive. He took after his father in certain lights and the O'Quinn lads were known throughout Kerry to be handsome. Along with the grey at his temples and throughout his natural brown hair, terms like *Silver Fox* had been thrown around.

Did he miss sex? Well, he was a red-blooded male. But what he missed more than that was the connection that grew over time. Random hookups or one night stands were not his thing.

"Mrs. McKeel," he began. "Thank you, but I'm not interested. If you are truly feeling poorly, I highly suggest going to see Doc Needlers."

He turned and promptly closed his eyes. The crazy woman had pulled her top off and the lace bra did little to cover her breasts.

"Please, put your clothes back on," he muttered. "I will send you my bill." He gathered his things and hurried toward the door. There would be as no bill, but he had to think of something to say.

"You don't want to make an enemy of me, O'Quinn," she called after him.

"I'll take my chances," he replied.

"I told you to give up your v-card to that one guy in University. That way you wouldn't have to worry about this," Geoffrey Ainsley said as he poured wine into his chic stemless glasses.

"I'm not giving *it* up for no reason," Corinne replied, tucking her left leg under her as she sat on his couch.

"And a hot guy isn't a valid reason?" He questioned, handing her the glass, and sitting beside her.

"Some of us aren't sluts," she answered, taking a large sip.

"Oh, harsh," he winced, teasingly. "But accurate." Corinne breathed a laugh. "I can't help it if I love my women."

"Mmhmm," she grinned. "Only women?" He gave her a sardonic look but didn't respond to her insinuation.

"You know I offered to... help you out with that little issue." He winked.

"And you and I agreed, we didn't want to ruin our friendship."

"Yeah, yeah," he replied. "Pity that."

"Besides, I don't think the estimable Lady Winifred Russell would appreciate it."

"Low blow, love," Geoff replied. "You know we don't even like each other."

"You could try, you know. She will be the future Lady Garvey, Mrs. Geoffrey Ainsley."

"Do I need reminding?" He questioned and took a large sip. "Ugh, this isn't strong enough for that conversation." He motioned to the wine.

"I still don't understand if you really don't want to agree to the betrothal, why you don't tell your father no."

"Have you tried saying no to the Earl of Torrington?"

"No, but if you don't love her..."

"Aristocratic marriages have nothing to do with love. An heir and a spare, and then we will be able to do our own thing. She's had lovers in the past I'm sure. She can have any she wants after my sons are born. So long as we're both discrete nothing should prevent us from living quite different lives. The only time we will need to see each other is when we have public events to attend."

"Have you talked to her about it?"

"Nope," he shook his head. "But it is the twenty-first century. So long as for the first two years or however long it takes to have two sons, she is loyal to me, I will be loyal to her. It's all very romantic."

"I'm sure," Corinne rolled her eyes. "Arranged marriages… what a pair we are."

"Hey, at least you'll be out of yours in five years," he teased.

"I'm serious, Geoff," she said, her voice catching.

"I know you are, sweetheart. I'm sorry. This isn't good. I'm just trying to make you laugh," he stated.

"I know, but I'm scared, Geoff. This is tantamount to prostitution and rape." She shook.

"It'll be all right. You stay here tonight or for however long you want," he placed an arm around her shoulders. She leaned her head against him.

"Thank you," she answered. "But I don't want you drawn into this. My father screwed up… again but this time it's unforgivable. I don't even think money will dissuade Rossi… not that I have any."

"You know I'd help," Geoff offered. "I'm not exactly Vanderbilt but I have some money. I'll even go talk to my father."

She looked up at him, "You'd do that for me?"

"Absolutely, I would do anything for you, love. Surely you know that by now."

Geoff's father, the renowned pacifist and tenth Duke of Torrington disowned his son when he enlisted in the latest war with the Middle East. Since Geoffrey's subsequent heroic career ended in an honorable medical discharge from Her Majesty's Army, Special Reconnaissance Division, his playboy and *laissez faire* attitude caused him to be in the news in various lights sparking controversary, questions of his sexuality, and causing scandals to wreck the name of Ainsley, all of which, his father detested.

Since he was an only child, he could not be disinherited, but his father had cut off his allowance. The duke tolerated Geoff for his mother's sake. But they were hardly friends.

"Thank you," she said. "But I would never want to force you to do that. I know how it would make you feel."

"You aren't forcing. I'm offering. He has connections," Geoff offered. "I'll at least talk to him."

Corinne nodded and kissed his cheek. They were silent for a long while just watching the flames on the gas fireplace jump and drinking their wine.

"I need to get away," she finally said. "Somewhere they won't find me."

"Like where?"

"I don't know, but if I'm not in London, maybe he won't come for me."

"You know Peter lives in America with his fiancée, but he has family in Ireland."

"Peter?" she questioned.

Geoff nodded. "You still keep in contact with him?"

"Of course, he's my best friend."

"I thought I was your best friend," she pouted teasingly.

"You're my best girl friend," he winked.

"You and he met in Afghanistan, right?"

"Yep," he took another sip of wine. "We were sent to find him. He had gotten himself captured. That was the beginning of our friendship. They're coming to stay with me when they travel to Europe for their honeymoon."

"Awe, that's generous of you," she replied.

"We were always friends," he justified. "And I'm glad he's found someone to love. Vivian's a nice girl… for an American."

She laughed at his quintessential English arrogance. "Isn't Peter American, too?" she questioned.

"All I'm saying is maybe try Ireland," he changed the subject. "It's beautiful. And desolate and separated by a sea. It could be perfect."

"I can't say I've ever been," she calculated the money in her savings. "Do you know how much it would be?"

"Don't worry about that," he answered. "I'll take care of it."

At that moment, Oscar, Corinne's Irish wolfhound padded over to her from the bed she set up in the guest room. He whined but knew Geoff's house rule. *No dog on the couch.*

She stroked her dogs head and scratched behind the ears. "I can't ask that of you," she said. "I'll find a way. I have always wanted to go see mum's homeland."

"Let's go tomorrow and open a joint account, my name as primary and that way I can put some money in there for you. I can also help by paying your bills while you're away."

"That's too much for you to do."

"Would you stop? It's not. Not for my girl," he answered, refilling her wine glass. "And besides, you have what? *Two* bills."

She conceded. "Okay, I would say no if I had a choice."

"I know you would. But that's what friends are for."

"I love you, Geoff."

"Love you too," he winked and clinked his glass to hers. "It'll be okay. I won't let anything happen to you."

Corinne took a sip and a deep breath. She rested her head on his shoulder, feeling his arm come around her and stared into the fireplace. Her body, mind, and heart heavy with thought and fear. Hopefully, if she closed her eyes, she could wish everything back to normal.

Made in the USA
Middletown, DE
15 September 2021